AIR FORCE BLUE

Assault from the Sky
GREGORY MARCEL

Gotham Books

30 N Gould St.
Ste. 20820, Sheridan, WY 82801
https://gothambooksinc.com/

Phone: 1 (307) 464-7800

© 2022 Gregory Marcel. All rights reserved.

No part of this book may be reproduced, stored in a retrieval system, or transmitted by any means without the written permission of the author.

Published by Gotham Books (November 4, 2022)

ISBN: 979-8-88775-130-6 (sc)
ISBN: 979-8-88775-131-3 (e)

Because of the dynamic nature of the Internet, any web addresses or links contained in this book may have changed since publication and may no longer be valid.

The views expressed in this work are solely those of the author and do not necessarily reflect the views of the publisher, and the publisher hereby disclaims any responsibility for them.

Table of Contents

CHAPTER 1
    Wilburton 5
CHAPTER 2
    South Side 16
CHAPTER 3
    Soldier Field 32
CHAPTER 4
    The Moment 47
CHAPTER 5
    The Warehouse 56
CHAPTER 6
    Champions 70
CHAPTER 7
    Good-bye Arthur 80
CHAPTER 8
    Mount Whitney 96
CHAPTER 9
    Adulthood 110
CHAPTER 10
    The Draft 120
CHAPTER 11
    The Takeover 126
CHAPTER 12
    Send in the Marines 139
CHAPTER 13
    G-Strings 149

CHAPTER 1
WILBURTON

"Come on, white boy! Come on, white boy! When I get finished with your ass, you are going to wish you were never born!" Larry viciously screamed through his mouthpiece during head-to-head contact drills. "I don't know you, but if you keep talking like that, you might just get a severe butt-kicking!" John barked back as he rammed Larry with the left-shoulder pad.

Wilburton Middle School had just been completed a year ago. Chicago needed this shot in the arm to help integrate the city plagued by racism. "Man, this summer heat with all my football gear doesn't feel too great, and to top it off, this ugly acting-black guy is trying to challenge me. I bet he's from South Side. Boy, his breath sure stinks." John couldn't believe this boastful punk.

"All right, boys, let's hit hard. When the season starts, there will be no room for momma's boys." Coach Gus Thompson half-jokingly screamed during the drills. The ex-Chicago Bears linebacker coach, who at fifty-seven couldn't coach at the pro level any longer after his use of language cost him his position, kept his players' intensity level high. One had to respect the coach, who stood six foot six and carried his 280 pounds well under the circumstances. And to top it off, Thompson resembled a grizzly bear that had been in a few scraps in its time. Coach

Thompson noticed two of his larger players trying to tear each other's necks off during the contact drills. Larry Williams, the cocky kid from the South Side, seemed to want to lead the team.

Williams stood six foot one and weighed 180 pounds. The mean streets of South Side gave Williams the permanent scowl. The slender but wide shoulders, the springy way he ran, the ebony skin, the close-cut coal black hair. With those penetrating acorn eyes, Williams was a natural for leadership.

Cade on the other hand was already known for his breakaway speed. At the weigh in, Coach noticed Cade, a five foot eight, 160-pound teenager, who could pass for a high schooler. "Ten seconds on the hundred-yard dash, man I love this kid!" Thompson was beside himself with glee, thinking of John's speed. "Hey, Williams, get over here!" Coach Thompson screamed.

"What up, Coach?" Williams got out between gasps.

"I thought you said you wanted to be a linebacker!" Thompson sneered.

"Shit, I will be, Coach," Williams proudly proclaimed.

"Look, son, you're six foot one and a hundred and eighty pounds, and you're letting little Johnny get the best of you, get in there and stick!" Thompson knew talent when he saw it. "All right, man," Larry angrily replied. Larry knew football was his ticket out of the mean streets. "Damn, white boys have it so easy, bet they are eating good too. Now this mutha Cade is trying to show me up. I'll be glad when this shit is over for the day, my arms are tired," Williams silently complained. Thompson then ordered his team, the Knight Hawks, to prepare for sprint drills. "All right, girls, I want every one to run this forty yards in under seven seconds. Ready, go!" The summer sessions were there to prepare the boys for the rough-and-tumble world of tackle football. During a break in the action, Coach Thompson yelled, "Keep it up, Larry, with that speed, you'll be a cinch to be a starter."

"You don't have to say nothing to me, Coach, I'm the shit around here!"

"Son, I like your effort, but with that attitude, you won't go far in my program. I run things for now nigger boy!" Coach knew these kids weren't crybabies. *With the language kids use now day's, it wouldn't surprise me if they laughed about this little incident in the showers,* Gus thought to himself. Gus underestimated Greydog! In seconds, Thompson was wrestling a six-foot-one, 180-pound tiger to the ground. "Easy, son, you have to learn the ropes around here. You have to learn to respect authority."

"Man, let me up, I will show your ass some authority!" Larry yelled as he spit grass out of his mouth. "You want to get up, here get up." The six-foot-six, 280-pound Thompson firmly but respectfully kept Williams off him. Cade, who noticed the skirmish, felt that Williams trained with the best of them, but he sure is a smart aleck. Sensing he had to do something, John yelled, "Come on, Williams, you're making it hard for everyone else." Williams, sensing the tide was turning, backed off Coach. *Damn, little bastard might make a fine football player someday,* Thompson mused to himself. After the first scrimmage, Coach let the young gladiators mingle. Every one on the squad knew of John Cade. His ability in grammar school track earned him recognition all over Chicago. A handsome fellow John, the jetblack hair, the naturally tanned skin, the budding muscles, some say he favored the starring actor Tom Laughlin in the famed movie *Billy Jack*. John would blush when girls would say that, but it made him feel good.

Yes, his grandpa, ever since John was old enough to remember, would tell stories of Will Cade, one of the few Indians in old Chicago who could get away with being seen publicly with a white woman. Will also happened to earn a decent living in banking. He never failed to let his generation know that the name Cade was something special and not to waste it. After John was finished impressing the team, talking about his speed, they all headed for the showers. Carolyn Jones, who felt she would be with John forever, patiently waited outside the school gates for her lifelong friend. Carolyn, turning thirteen the past June, was wearing her favorite summer attire. Blue plaid Bermuda shorts with the white calypso shirt. A reserved teen, Carolyn loved not being in the spotlight yet for some reason felt gregarious around John.

The old Seward Park had been used to build Wilburton Middle School. John's parents insisted he go to a public school system so he wouldn't fear other races. On the way to the school gates, John noticed Carolyn, so he said his good-byes to all the guys on the team who admired him, who they considered to be big John. Carolyn, a youthful thirteen, was still in braces yet one couldn't help but appreciate the soft and beautiful way she carried herself. The soft blue almond-shaped eyes, the natural pouting lips. She kept John from losing his composure by reminding him of his manly obligation upon entering the uncharted waters of intercourse. "Hey, Carolyn, how long have you been waiting?" John playfully asked. "Not long," Carolyn answered as she winked at John. Before John could comment, out of nowhere popped Larry. "Hey, punk!" Larry sneered, moving ever closer to John. "I'm waiting for you to kick my ass like you said." Totally ignoring the passersby, Larry sucker punched John on the jaw, hoping to knock him out. The force of the blow swayed John, but he never left his feet. Instinctively, Carolyn stepped over to Larry and slapped Larry out of anger. In a dirty smile, Larry backhanded Carolyn. Screaming in pain by the force of the blow, Carolyn tumbled to the ground. Larry menacingly stood over Carolyn and let out a hoarse chuckle. John, who knew Chicago was a place where fighting was common, never thought he'd see the day when somebody struck Carolyn. With the roar of a lion, John rushed Larry; and John, oblivious to any onlookers, caught Larry off guard. He then placed his right hand between Larry's legs, his left hand on Larry's right shoulder. Then, with the strength of two men, John lifted Larry over his head and slammed him to the ungiving sidewalk. Furious, Larry popped right up and quickly reached into his Levis and pulled out a pocketknife. Opening the blade, Larry yelled, "Come and get this bitch!" John, angry now, growled as he took up his best impression of a heavyweight fighter. The two faced each other. Larry realizing if he cut John with the four-inch blade, his football days would be over. He backed off, but still wielding the knife, Larry took several steps back away from John; and in front of startled onlookers, he sprinted toward Oak Street. With a furrowed brow, Carolyn spoke through stomach flutters. "John, I'm scared. What if he tries that again?" John studied Carolyn. The shoulder-length mahogany hair, the smiling eyes. Carolyn was past puberty; the precious breasts were waiting for a wandering hand. The hips were beginning to spread, yet his belief in God's arrangement for marriage made John realize he'd violate her innocence. Carolyn, reading John's mind, stated smilingly, "What you looking at, Johnny?" Happily startled, John stated, "Just the most gorgeous girl this side of Chicago."

"Oh yeah," Carolyn playfully shot back, "well then, who's the prettiest in the whole city if I'm not?"

Not to be outdone, John got out, "Your mom of course." Carolyn blushed.

Barbara Cade explained to her son that she didn't mind the drive back and forth from their high-rise apartment on near Northside to Wilburton. When John noticed his mom coming, he explained to Carolyn, "If you mention this to my mom, she'll probably want me to transfer for my seventh grade year, so *mums* the word okay, Carolyn, my pet."

"Oh, all right," Carolyn moaned. Barbara, a conscious woman who believed in the Bible first, was surprised to see Carolyn with John. A five-foot-six, shapely woman, Barbara never failed to turn heads. The forty-inch hips, the slim waist, the wrinkle-free complexion, the caramel-colored eyes. At thirty-seven, she still kept men drooling to spend time with her. Barbara had known Carolyn for a good part of the young lady's life. Barbara sighed as she patted her auburn hair, which was tightly pinned and formed a ball on the top. As she eyed the two teens together, Barbara started thinking about the situation. "She sure makes a good friend to John. They've known each other for so long, I hope they're not sleeping together yet. Lord knows I'm too young to be a grandmother!" As the smooth-running new yellow white '93 Coupe de Ville pulled up, Barbara noticed the left side of Carolyn's face was cherry red. While the two climbed in to the front seat, Barbara, concerned, asked Carolyn what had happened. Carolyn made up a story that she had run into some young street thugs who tried to rob her, but since she didn't have much money, they roughed her up a little bit but that John arrived and chased them off. Mrs. Cade questioned John, "Is this true, son?" John's hesitating answer of yes mom gave Barbara the impression that John wasn't being totally honest, but she accepted his feeble compliance.

Dinner that night was quiet. The two baked chickens with peas, rice, and homemade biscuits didn't last long. "John, you sure do have an appetite this evening," Barbara curiously asked while pointing a finger toward the plate where the chicken formally resided. "Leave him alone, dear, that sport he loves so much probably leaves him famished." Harold knew his son John would grow up to be a strapping young man. John reminded Harold of Will Cade, his great-great-grandfather. John was considered Caucasian, but that Indian blood, Apache, coursed through his veins. Harold, a youthful forty-two, took after his great-great-grandmother's side of the family, the white ancestry. Yet he carried the name Cade proudly. The sandy brown hair, the ever-so-slight bulge around the tummy, the pleasant green eyes. Harold stood six foot one and weighed a little over 190 pounds. One would never fathom the drive behind one of the finest business lawyers in Chicago. The vicelike handshakes always let one know that Harold meant business.

After dinner, the family would love to sit in the living room facing the sparkling Lake Michigan and let dinner settle. The duplex apartment had three spacious bedrooms, a beautiful hand-designed kitchen, two full deluxe toilet rooms, and a perfect view of the lake. The richly designed apartment was lavishly decorated, from the antique but expensive paintings to the bearskin rug in the middle of the floor, which had been passed down generations through Harold's side of the family.

As four o'clock rolled around, John decided he wanted to visit Lincoln Park. "Dad, is it okay if I go to Lincoln Park?"

"Be careful, son," Harold admonished.

"I will, Dad," John lovingly replied to the man of the house, and after giving his mom a peck on the cheek, John left the five-story high-rise apartment. He then took the elevator, a valuable addition to the building, downstairs. Once there, he used a first-floor pay phone to call a cab. "Boy, my twenty-dollar-a-day allowance sure comes in handy at times," John silently thanked his father. Lincoln, the largest park in Chicago, had an assortment of activity for a Monday evening. The sea of faces filled the park. The smiling children, the overworked parents, the tourist, what a way to relax. Knowing the zoo well, John decided to forego that and the bathing beaches and headed for the conservatory. He loved the palm house, especially viewing the giant palms. John sometimes did this for hours, but today, he only wanted to quickly restore his peace of mind. "Man, I love this city," John thought aloud. He replayed his fantasy in his mind. *If I could, someday, I'd love to help in keeping violence off the streets, so the public could be safe. Even the mayor Mr. Daley seems sick of all the crime. This city has also seen its share of illegal activity,* John pondered. John thought of all the gangsters in the Windy City, *Capone stood out. That guy Williams, when he becomes an adult, I wonder will he be in a gang.* John kept visualizing his favorite dream. Ever since he could remember, he'd envision his toy jets and soldiers from his vast toy collection mounting machine guns blazing away at lawbreakers. "I bet no one would take me serious, if anything, helicopters would be used, but they're so cumbersome. The pilot will have to shoot quick unless they used cobras, then the rear end of the helicopter would be vulnerable. But my dreams would allow soldiers to be at every angle and pinpoint their targets. I bet that would keep the enemy scrambling." Snapping back to reality, John thought, after some thirty minutes of browbeating in the conservatory, that he'd seen enough for the day. When he arrived home, Harold asked John did he want to see the Cubs tonight. "You know, son, it hasn't been very long since lights were installed at Wrigley." John paused in the doorway, then added, "Who's playing tonight, Dad?"

"Cubs and Mets, son, seven-thirty start." John thought about this then nodded. The family was dressed in their summer attire. Harold and Barbara wore cutoff shorts, and both put on their worn, comfortable cross trainers with no socks.

John felt comfortable in his blue Adidas jumpsuit that he'd worn to football practice. It was tailored too for his liking, knee-high. The floppers he had slipped into after dinner would do as far as his feet were concerned. Once the family started out of the apartment and on the way to Wrigley Field, Barbara and John would love to look at the many spectacular sights of Chicago. The romantic waters of Lake Michigan and the beautiful lit-up skyscrapers always excited the Cades.

With heavy traffic, which didn't bother Harold who was used to thinking while driving, Harold pondered over his assignments as a business lawyer. Things were going well for McDugal Enterprises. The tennis shoe giant far exceeded Harold's dream as far as his personal financial needs were concerned. His love for John and his son's desire to succeed made the hard work pay off. The six odd years of toiling at Harvard prepared Harold well for the vicious world of Eastern American business tactics. The family, through Will Cade, had a small fortune of stocks and bonds. Harold used a fourth of his inheritance to pay for his education at the Ivy League institution. Meeting Barbara while on vacation in Australia after the bar exam, the two never took their eyes off each other. The drive, taking a little longer than usual because of traffic, eased Harold back to the present.

Parking, always a hassle at game time, gave Harold fits. The throng of people at the ballpark kept the family huddling together while they scurried to the ticket booth. "The cheap seats would have to do for tonight," Harold suggested to the dismay of Barbara and John. "Come on, Dad, have some heart," John feigned with a hint of sarcasm. Barbara scolded Harold, "Remember, dear, there's no cushion on those seats."

Harold, undaunted, shot back, "I know, but this isn't the World Series, not yet anyway, you two!" The family grumbled along to the cheap seats. Some thirty minutes later, they were settled in. The first pitch had already been tossed. John liked baseball, but it would never come close to his love for tackle football.

The solid crack of the bat turned John's head. The flight of the ball carried high into the night. Finally, it settled three to four feet over the left-field fence. The roar of the crowd could only mean one thing—Cubs home run. "Daydreaming has caused me to miss so many things," John fretted, pulling at his eyebrow in frustration. "Darn, I didn't even catch who hit it."

About the only other interesting thing to John was the seventh-inning stretch song sang with the legendary Cubs broadcaster Harry Caray, who sang with the melody of a duck, but his love for the team was unabashed. John even hummed along to the unusual event. On the way home, Barbara, unlike herself, aired her complaints. "Honey, let's watch something on television the next time you get an itch for entertainment." Feeling hurt at Barbara's resentment, Harold, while driving, gave his wife a look of uneasy puzzlement then added, "Sweetheart, being cooped up in the apartment doesn't actually get the ole juices flowing if you know what I mean, we had our fun. We even got to see Rhino hit one out." John leaned forward in the backseat of the sedan and with anticipation said, "That was Rhino, Dad!"

"Sure was, son," Harold said, nodding in the process while steering his way through traffic, anxious to get home. Traffic eased, the family then hit Oak Street and cruised toward home. The well-lit Victorian apartments reminded Harold he had a choice among the luxuriously built high-rise apartments on the gold coast. His quarter-million-dollar salary eased any doubts as to what Harold could afford for his family. The family said their goodnights. Once in his bedroom, John became reminiscent. The toy air force display in the left-hand corner of the extremely spacious, comfortably designed room really touched John. It was a perfect reflection off the deep blue walls. Every night, before going to sleep, John would visualize his dream of taking back America. If only people could see there's no solution to solving a crime victim's losses, whether it's property or a loved one.

Barbara and Harold, as usual for the past thirteen years, came and gave John the final family free time together. With John busy with school and football and father, Harold, spending so much time with travel assignments for McDugal, these moments meant a lot to every one. When John was born, Barbara and Harold decided to let John sleep by himself, as young as possible—old Cade family ritual. "You awake, son?" Harold asked through the door. "Sure, come on in, Mom and Dad," John knowingly answered. As the dark brown walnut varnish-free door opened, Harold and Barbara entered the room.

The family all took their positions. With Harold holding hands with the two of them, they all bent down on their knees, forming a triangle. Harold then led the family in prayer.

CHAPTER 2
SOUTH SIDE

Chicago had decided to revamp its public school system. With all the crimes and alarming rise in the population, the city decided to build twelve new schools ranging from grade seventh through eighth. This way, the preteens would have a change. Gangs constantly threatened to take their share, so the broad-shouldered powerhouse had to save its future. The state-of-the-art schools were a blessing to those who were poor—the blacks, the Latinos, and also the immigrants who were new to Chicago. This was the target—get those children educated the right way.

It took twelve years, but the eight-hundred-million-dollar project was a success. The kids were already having full contact drills. If they could now survive the brutal winters, the workers withstood while building the beautiful institutions. The twenty-three construction workers, who lost their lives when the first floor of one of the buildings collapsed in 1981, would really appreciate the architectural improvement.

Larry Williams picked the Nighthawks of Wilburton over all others because of the publicity. John Cade, even though not a proven talent, had middle school scouts flaming with complements. Larry silently tipped his hat to John. "Gotta give him credit, he's doing it." But it was frustrating for Larry to deal with the white man and his laws. It mentally tore him to pieces at times. His father, JoJo Williams, who in the seventies lived the life of the old-school gangster, was killed when Larry was an infant. After that, Larry's mother left him with his grandmother Wilma, who one morning opened the door because of a noise, and there was Larry.

JoJo was Wilma's only son. A hardened but bright young man, JoJo served two years in the National Guard as a cook. After being caught for armed robbery at the age of twenty-three, JoJo was discharged immediately, getting a two-year suspended sentence because of no prior convictions. After the trial, no more than one hundred feet from the courthouse, JoJo was laced by a passing vehicle. No suspects were ever found. Many believed it was the family of the victims who were robbed. Larry hated hearing that story; it made him feel worse about his life at this stage. But Wilma would always let her only grandchild know, "It's not what you do to survive in this world that will get you killed. It's messing with folks' property, remember that, son." The Georgian accent would always be hidden by Wilma, but she dragged some words and left off the proper ending on so many others. "Just to hard messing with those white folks words," was a favorite line of Wilma's. She had been going to English classes for five years and had just begun learning what grammar actually meant. Yet at seventy-three, she missed a little too much of the structure of English during her teen years. Still, she would read to Larry every night. Wilma would say it was to soften Larry's hard head. "Boy, you are destined to tear up something," Grandma always teased Larry, but Larry's mind was on other things. "Damn, every day waking up in this dump," Larry yelled as he awakened. "I should get into the crack game," Larry chided himself as he threw the covers back. "But I'd do too much time for it, gotta stay legal." Larry knew whatever happened,

Wilburton and its high profile could only help him so much. He checked the time after scrambling out of bed. "Eleven thirty! Better get moving."

Tuesday, leaving the apartment, Larry felt fine after yesterday's practice. On his way back to Wilburton for another session, Larry met his three protégés, Juanita, Quenlin, and Sharkey. The 2:00 p.m. weather was a tick under seventy, cool for a late July day. The four Wilburton students walked down the crowded and rugged streets of South Side. This hapless section, with the ghetto-stricken apartments and trash all over what was once the sidewalk, failed to stir up disgust any longer.

Once inside a local pool hall, the trio looked at Larry. "How much time you have before practice, Greydog!" Sharkey roughly barked out in his post-adolescent voice. The place was known as Seal's, named after the owner Seal, a dark thin man with a glass eye. Seal didn't care how old his customers were as long as cash was served. The crowd would scare a seasoned policeman at this hour, and not to mention the filth, but everyone respected JoJo and his. Sharkey, a friend of Larry's ever since he could remember, was the one responsible for giving Larry the name Greydog in the second grade because of a gray poodle. He never saw Larry come in Seal's without ordering a beer. Sharkey, thirteen, hadn't grown into a size he liked in order to compete in school sports. "Negro have to be a damn giant," Sharkey always teased himself. The light brown skin and curly black hair gave Sharkey a distinct advantage when it came to the ladies. His perfectly arranged soft features and medium-sized lips gave girls the impression that Sharkey was half-white. This irritated Sharkey to no end, but the magical feel the bitches gave his heart made him want to chase them forever.

Sharkey never worried much about Larry until two weeks ago, Larry's big day at Wilburton. In Sharkey's understanding, Larry's version of the story, on the way home from practice, Larry met Arthur X, the two talked of forming a gang, and Larry went for it like white on rice. Sharkey, still mentally putting the pieces together, couldn't get over Larry's future recruiting efforts, as Larry would say, "Intellect over brawn and all races." Sharkey, still thinking of Larry's story, went on. "How the hell is he going to get white people following him, and to top that, he wants only smart niggers. Their parents would be all over the phone dialing the 'Man' on Larry's ass!"

"Hey, Sharkey, quit daydreaming and shoot some pool, nigger!" Larry then motioned to the only empty pool table in the seedy joint and yelled, "I have time for one game, and you know what else? Your two whores has left, and like my daddy said," Larry then sang out, "'There's no use in looking back, son, because Jody's has your Cadillac.'" Larry ordered a beer. He drank the ice-cold thirty-two ounce Budweiser quickly. Realizing the time, Larry exclaimed, "Shit! Let's go, man. Damn, I'm going to be late." They quickly threw the pool sticks on the table and ran out of the crowded Seal's. They spotted Quenlin and Juanita, who were waiting down the street, holding a cab. The driver, a Hungarian immigrant, was a small thin man but wiry with a quick tongue. The graying hair gave him the American look. But the weak blood of being small-boned for Hungarian stood out. "Would you hurry it up!" Hermie was becoming impatient.

"Would you wait, bastard, shit!" Juanita yelled, snarling at Hermie. Hermie was not quite sure what was being said, knowing only enough of this sick American language for the taxi business. His parents warned him, but with the scowl he was getting from the young black girl in this part of the city, Hermie could only hunch his shoulders.

"Hey, get in the freaking cab!" Larry yelled as he came sprinting out of Seal's. Larry jumped in the front seat. Once Larry and Sharkey had noticed the girls standing by the taxi as they left Seal's, Larry quickly told Sharkey of an area where the four could escape without paying. Larry would then meet them later that day after practice. The beer was starting to feel good to Larry. While he watched Hermie wheeling the taxi, he hummed the tune, "Beer a day will keep the doctor away." Hermie's senses had alerted him when Larry entered the vehicle. "You pay up front, eh?" Hermie sheepishly held out his hand.

"We pay when we get all right," Larry gave Hermie the look only oppression could produce. Hermie shamefully looked away from Larry then agreed. "Okay, you pay when you go." Larry began noticing the females; he'd known Quenlin since she and her mother moved into the building next to the Williams's apartment almost six years ago. They had sex several times, but Larry's aggressiveness scared Quenlin. Larry was in love with Quenlin.

Her shoulder-length almost-red hair went well with her high yellow complexion. The upturned nose, the big but soft lips, the tight round ass! When she wanted to, she could seduce almost any man, but Larry had plans for her. Larry turned his attention to Juanita. She hung onto Sharkey like a tick. She could pass for a nigger Olive Ole. Bitch was skinnier than a toothpick, wore a wig and liked to spend money, and was only twelve. Sharkey yelled out, "Coming up on Chicago Avenue," which brought Larry out of his sexual fantasies.

Turning to the driver, Larry yelled, "Stop here!" Pulling over to the curb, the cab came to a halt. Larry gave Sharkey time to escort the ladies out of the cab. He then grabbed Hermie by the neck, and with one swift motion, Larry sucker punched Hermie on the bridge of the nose. The Hungarian, scraping for every dollar, wasn't about to let some young black punk take his money. But someone wasn't being fair, where did the lights go? And with that, Hermie slouched over in the driver's seat.

Cautious of onlookers, Larry took his time so as not to draw attention to himself. He got into the till over four hundred dollars. Larry decided that amount was enough. He then checked the fare; it read forty-three dollars. Larry laughed to himself. Before he exited the checker, Larry muttered, "How the hell was that going to be paid, silly broads." Sharkey had watched everything in amazement. He said nothing as Larry coolly ushered the three away from the car, and an unconscious Hermie and walked them toward the north of Huron Street. Once they got away from the neighborhood where they left the checker, they all let out a sigh of relief. As they continued walking, the checker flew past them. Hermie, not aware who was watching him, seemed to want to just get the hell out of the area. Sharkey, curious, had to ask, "How much you get, Greydog? I need some money to get these girls back home." Larry pulled out the bills. Sharkey gasped; Larry shot him a keep-your-mouth-shut look to those back home. He then deftly counted seven twenties.

"Take this and get on the trolley, and don't mess with any more cabs," Larry scorned his friend. He then added, "You are not the dog, Sharkey!" Young Sharkey let out an exasperated, "Damn it, I won't!" Larry then grabbed Quenlin by the arm; she tried snatching it away. "Leave me alone, Larry," she whined, "you are always hurting people." Hurt by the bitter statement, Larry quickly reminded her, "You took the money, girl, shit!" Not to be outdone, Quenlin put her hands on her hips and defiantly said, "Shit, nigger! How else am I going to clean my pussy!" Larry, catching the jest of the whole thing, roared. After straightening up, Larry excused himself. "I have to go, gang." He then gave Sharkey the chi-town dap, playfully punched Juanita, pecked Quenlin, and headed for the gates of Wilburton. Larry had the halls all to himself as he walked toward the locker room. Remembering the incident with the cab driver angered Larry; he thought of Sharkey. "Told Sharkey to keep walking, damn, he let my bitch see that now she will play scared for real on me." Then, sensing the time, Larry wondered how late he was.

As he arrived in the locker room, Larry was glad it was empty. The rather tidy shower room made things comfortable for the teens. They could shower right after practice or the games that would be played at Wilburton. The new facility hadn't been there long enough to get the usual odor of the sweat and funk of men at play. Darting his eyes back and forth, Larry noticed the large round standard clock; time stood out on the whitewashed walls of the gymnasium. "Four thirty-seven, damn! Now this fool-ass coach is going to drop on my ass!" The noise seemed to be on loudspeakers as Larry clanged his locker, desperately trying to open it. Before Larry got his shoulder pads on, Coach Thompson entered. Gus eyed Williams; Larry didn't notice Coach. "Stop right there, Williams! I've been hearing things, and they don't look good." Gus went on, "I'll tell you right now, Williams, you have talent, but I'm no one's alibi, you get that!" Gus then calmly approached Larry, and with his off hand, his left, gut punched Greydog! Without a blink, Gus ordered Larry to get ready for practice. When the air hit Larry's lungs, he almost screamed. The knot wouldn't go away. Gasping for air and doubling over as much as possible to minimize the pain, Larry finally dressed.

There was no way Larry was going to let Coach see how hard he had hit him. "Shit, I'm joggin' out on the field."

The elaborate setup had natural grass and bleachers. Each middle school, under the new rules, would seat one thousand people to help offset the eight hundred million dollars it took to construct the learning centers. The winter months would determine how hungry parents would be when it came to supporting their children.

Williams had made it to the field to witness Coach barking out a drill. The boys were in full gear, rolling from left to right, then assuming the push-up position. A grueling task, yet the teens were ready. Ten minutes passed, Larry could feel the desire in Coach, and it shook Williams. The glare Coach gave Larry as Thompson barked commands at the Nighthawks would have ran most people away, but Larry held eye contact. The beer, still effective, had Larry wondering why he didn't vomit when Coach punched him. The pain had slowly gone away, yet it left Larry weak at the knees. Finally, Coach called for a break, "Get in there, Williams, one more late practice and I want twenty laps." Relieved, Larry responded, "Okay, Coach." After thirty minutes of hitting the practice dummies, Coach Thompson finally ordered ten laps around the football field.

As he watched his team hit the laps, Thompson mulled over the situation. "Boy, this school project may just go to the limit. These kids sure want to compete, man, first class equipment, own stadiums. I wonder what the other bums are doing with their kids." Then Coach turned his attention to Larry. "That damn Williams, if I ever hear about the bastard and another taxi, I'll for sure let the law have him."

The two and one half miles seemed to take forever. Being as bunched up as possible while jogging, the Nighthawks began to voice their opinions. Tony Ventura, a Mexican American, also the center, who stood five foot four and weighed a hefty 150 pounds. At thirteen, he already possessed a mustache and sideburns. Tony scolded the quarterback, Harmon Orosco, who at fifteen stood six feet and carried his 140-pound frame well.

He was perfect for quarterback. "Next time I snap you the ball, Harm, twitch when you want the ball, I can feel your hands and arms touching my ass!" This brought a tremendous amount of laughter from the thirty-eight members of the squad. "Knock it off, people, Coach is keeping a close watch on us." The respect John held silenced the Nighthawks. Larry, feeling nauseous from the beer, was barely able to keep the sarcasm from seeping out. Yet the thoughts roared, *Man, this fool must think he owns us, he's not the coach's son. I have to stay low though, think Coach know about that taxi, but shit I need to leave Cade alone might just overdue shit.* The loud shrill of the whistle guided the team back to Thompson. "Gather around, men." Thompson then informed Wilburton that the first scrimmage game would be against the Razorblades of Northside.

Of all middle schools, the old North Park gave the cotton Razorblades the glamour image of the whole program. The location was perfect. John, not wanting to be around the snobby rich kids, relished the idea of playing against some of the guys from his neighborhood. Thompson further instructed his players, "Girls, this city must really like kids because listen up, we're playing at Soldier Field. We'll be playing August 3, Wednesday, at 4:00 p.m. Next time I want to see any Nighthawks in my scarlet red practice jerseys is a week from today, right here at 2:30 p.m." Thompson, in his voice of authority went on, "You kids, for the past two weeks have withstood every challenge I've thrown at you. I'll let you learn from contact during the game. Remember, no spearing, men, you could easily hurt your opponent or yourself. Before we do our push-ups for the day, I'll remind you, dirty uniforms and towels go in my large hamper, not on the beautiful new floor provided by the city of Chicago. Assume the position!" For the seemingly one thousandth time, the teens felt the burning sensation ten sets of fifteen per set would do for a young arm.

As Coach released the team for the showers, he stared at Larry the whole time. Larry, sheepishly avoiding eye contact, sprinted toward the locker room. "Hey, Cade, you want to switch places? I'd love to be running back at game time."

"No, Myers, we want to win, remember?" John jokingly shot out. Alvin Myers, the left side linebacker, who at fourteen could already bench press 250 pounds. The 170-pound body solidified Wilburton's linebackers. To Alvin Myers, a homely looking fellow with acne, yet who had the winning smile, felt Cade was the best of the best and a good friend who didn't mind going out of his way.

The last shower was turned off. In silent unison, the young men seemed to thank taxpayers for sparing them the torture of being exposed to the older kids. Larry, one of twelve African Americans on the team, showered quickly. He was the first to leave the locker room. He left the school gates heading for Chestnut Street. He quickly, in his gangster style, walked down Michigan Avenue until he got to the Illinois central station, where he caught the train.

At six thirty, Larry stood on the corner of 103rd Street. Arthur X was waiting. "Greydog!" Arthur sang out. After the hug and greeting, the two shook hands Chicago style. Then in a low tone, yet the depth wouldn't leave, Arthur stood with his shoulders back with a you-can't-stop-me attitude with the way his arms dangled as he walked and said to Larry, "All praise to revolt, to hell with oppression!" Larry, attracted to the theory, as the two walked gave a second motion, "All praise to revolt, Arthur!" The two continued to walk on 103rd. The large metal constructed warehouse stood there waiting. "See, Greydog, I am not bullshitting. I can support you my brother, get that motion I told you about started. Shit, nigger, playing ball and shit, you could definitely recruit some serious people."

"Yes, but, Arthur, damn a gang? What about the man?"

"Listen, my young warrior. Every day I wake up," Arthur was careful not to look around whole he spoke, "something tells me it's my turn. Whitey isn't playing fair. He's not going to move over, so we have to take it."

"Arthur," Larry felt jittery, "man, I don't want to die, but living in that dump with Grandma is just like being dead." Arthur patted Larry on the back. "Listen, brother, I met a man named Terran. He's loaded, and he's from the Middle East. Don't tell anyone about it, Larry. I remember your father and you remind me of him. I can't do what you can to start a gang, but if you take America, I will be free. Now, Terran is going to pay for operating functions of this warehouse; everything's ready, so start recruiting babe!"

"Right on X. Shit, Greydog won't let you down." Larry headed for the train station. Arthur X watched Larry walk away. "That's going to be somebody, I can feel it!" Arthur who, at thirty-seven had spent ten years in prison while in Mississippi for killing the three men who attempted to rob him during a visit there with his father, could not forgive the structure. The Five Percenters, whom Arthur X had met serving his time, had taught George Smith, Arthur's slave name, how to survive in prison. During those years, Arthur became a scholar. He forced himself to physically train. The push-ups, the sit-ups, the chain gang. His warped viewpoint on justice made the theories of the Percenters more volatile. A statuesque man, Arthur weighed 240 pounds. The rugged weatherworn face gave X a mature look. He could pass for fifty or more years of age. The twenty-inch biceps, the washboard stomach, and forty-eight inch chest told another tale. The coal black skin and bald head gave Arthur such a primitive look; one wouldn't hesitate to avoid him if you met him on the streets and didn't know him. Arthur X walked back to the warehouse. He unlocked the door, and the large structure of dull gray tin and steel came to life when Arthur switched on the power. The white-painted barrels were there, all sixty of them. The round black spots painted all over them reminded Arthur of JoJo's military stories back in the old days. Arthur shed a tear, thinking of the seventies. "Damn, it was bad then." Arthur negatively went into the past, and he then thought with anguish, "But damn, it doesn't have shit on today!" The memories of he and JoJo filled Arthur's mind. As terrible as poverty was, Arthur still enjoyed the seemingly innocent adolescent years.

Terran, as the Americans called him, didn't mind financing this person's, who called himself X, idea of having a militia gang consisting of teenagers. Terran, whose family owned oil wells in Iraq, felt good that he happened to meet this Arthur X by chance through an American business associate when Arthur was looking for a job. Terran instantly took a liking to the big man, Mr. X, who always called Terran brother of oppression. The eighty-million-dollar fortune he possessed grew constantly. Having to learn to live quietly until his plans for seizing the Bay Area coast in California was complete. "If I could just keep the American authorities busy with these people, Mr. X will train, until my people can get through with the nuclear warheads." Terran's country wanted to destroy enough of the United States to consider her to cripple to be reinforced by the population, if a war were to break out in the Middle East. They didn't want America butting in. "This is perfect, the black wants to fight his own government, if they could be successful getting volunteers." Terran doubted it would happen, but in America, anything was possible. The city of Chicago, however, scared Terran. The murders, the loudness, the outright cockiness of the people made Terran crave for home. "I can't let my people down. For years Amerdica," as Terran pronounced it, "has wiped her butt in our faces, for decades. Now she will crawl." Terran could think of no other way to silence the powerful Americans.

"Hey, you all right, Tee?" Arthur X asked. Arthur was always worried about his Turkish friend. *Turkish or whatever, money is money,* Arthur reminded himself.

"Yes, Mr. X, I'm fine, just deep in thought." After a moment, Arthur excused himself. "Okay, well, I'm turning in for the night."

"Sure." Terran pleasantly smiled at Arthur then added, "See you in three weeks." The two embraced and then shook hands. Arthur saluted Terran and headed out of the warehouse and on to the streets of 103rd. *Man! Fool sitting in his empty ass office in the dark scares me,"* Arthur implied to himself while waiting for his ride home. Lisa Brown, Arthur's fiancée and a lawyer, pulled over. "Hey, baldy, you need a ride?" Arthur, realizing this was Lisa's way of relaxing him, responded, "I sure do, missy ma'am," Arthur, in his good-boy routine, responded, "Could you kindly gives a boy a ride?"

"Yes, but you're riding in the back, negras!" They both laughed in unison at the well-rehearsed lines they never tired themselves of hearing. Lisa, who grew up in Upstate New York, met Arthur while in Mississippi. After representing Arthur in court and losing, Lisa promised to stay in touch with George

Smith, Arthur's slave name at the time of his arrest, until his release from prison.

Lisa was mesmerized by the sheer mental growth of George over the ten-year period he spent in prison. His sheer prowess was what attracted Lisa to X. "If Dad found out I loved a nigger, he'd have a fit," Lisa always lamented. Arthur, who peddled marijuana for money, couldn't figure Lisa out. "Woman could be with anybody, why she hanging around my ass! Probably because of the money she knows Terran is capable of getting his hands on."

Terran had already given Arthur 250,000 dollars. Arthur now rested financially. His customers that he catered the marijuana to mainly consisted of white-collar workers, since the pair resided in a middle-level income area near Lake Shore Drive. Arthur, deep in thought, visualized Terran as he got in the front seat of Lisa's '64 Mustang, gold with a white hardtop. All original except for the dual exhaust. Arthur was in love with the economical strength of the thing. Terran, who was a small man with a brown complexion, had the customary full beard for a person of his ethnic background. The curly hair gave Terran the rabbinic look. Arthur couldn't get over the heavy accent. "That's one son of a gun I have never saw in jeans and T-shirts." He reminded Arthur of a Mexican, but that accent was definitely Eastern. "I bet he's in his fifties." Arthur then switched his attention to Lisa, his best friend as well as lover.

Her blonde hair, which she kept cut at the shoulders, always smelled of honey shampoo. A bit on the chubby side, she was at least two hundred pounds; but that mind of hers and those thoughtful light brown eyes, she looked a good forty-two. "Hey, Leece," Arthur, worried, asked, "what took you so long getting to the warehouse?" Lisa eyed her friend before she spoke. "I made dinner first, then I'd come and pick you up, Arthur, and we'd share a romantic meal together." Author's tummy gave him the feel of delicious food going down. "You are a sweet woman, Lisa B, I owe you big," Arthur said while eyeing Lisa dart through traffic. Lisa, feeling the love for Arthur, let him see her jealousy. "Just don't spend money on any other woman, and we'll be fine." Lisa then shot Arthur a knowing look.

"I got you, girl." Arthur then averted eye contact by looking out of the passenger's window at the brilliant scenery of Chicago. The ride went smoothly with the aid of the sounds. The sixties music on Lisa's compact disc player had the two spellbound. It reminded them of Mississippi. "Hey, Arthur, want to go see a movie tonight?" Angered over Lisa's memory lapse, Arthur frowned at Lisa as he raised his voice. "I don't want to be screwing around fighting no white boys over you, girl, all right!" Not looking at Arthur while she tried to brush off her hurt feelings, Lisa could only feebly get out. "Sorry, I forgot, Arthur." Arthur, sensing he was getting too rough on his girl apologized. "It's okay, Lisa." He then gave Lisa a reassuring pat on the leg. Lisa playfully warned her man, "Careful, you may cause us to speed up." Arthur howled at his lady's humorous side then added, "Quit it, Lisa. By the way, how's things going on your new case?"

"Not good, I'm doing research, and our client seems to have sticky fingers, if you know what I mean." Lisa eyed Arthur to see if he understood. Arthur could only say, "Sort of." Lisa went on, "Anyway, he's paying my firm two million, and it's all legit, so he's definitely done his homework. Anyway, the judge wants two years probation, but my client wants a clean slate." Arthur let it be known, his ignorance, "What did he do?" Lisa went on, "Supposedly, he ripped his company off for ten million big ones and destroyed the records, and since his family is rich and vouches for him, they can't prove the money in the account is stolen." Arthur whistled then added, "Who is this guy, James Bond?" Lisa smiled at Arthur. "No, some rich white guy whose family is loaded. He's a businessman."

Arthur finally caught on. "Oh, so he used his family to shield his thievery."

"Very clever, Mr. X." With the car garage coming up, Lisa wheeled the Mustang inside. Finding her spot rather quickly, the two then got out of the car. This was the worst of times about living here, the muggers waiting for an opportunity. Arthur never relished fighting, but this was the time in life he liked being big. Lisa slid her hand into her purse to the nickel-plated specially designed .32 caliber. "Never can be too sure, Art," Lisa's favorite nickname for Arthur. "I'm glad I'm on your side, babe." Once inside the apartment, Arthur's mind drifted to Larry. "Boy said a young white boy slammed him to the concrete. Maybe have to sic one of my boys on him. Larry wants to handle it, so I'll leave it alone." Lisa came over to Arthur X, and the two embraced. The sparsely designed room still showed class; everything was top of the line. Dinner felt good to Arthur. He ate four helpings of the shrimp gumbo and French bread. The brandy, while eating, had Arthur in love with his two tons of fun white woman. Deep in thought, Arthur floated back to Larry. *Hope he can start recruiting. He has to do something.* As ten thirty rolled around, the two were in bed, braced in intercourse. Their minds, for the moment, were in a pleasurable oblivion.

CHAPTER 3
SOLDIER FIELD

The city of Chicago showed its enthusiasm. Over forty-three thousand paid the three-dollar gate fee to view the young men battle. Gus Thompson relished the fact that the Nighthawks were the home team. They would use the Bears' locker room. With Gus having so many connections here in Chicago, one had to wonder, was this a publicity thing?

Cade couldn't shake the butterflies. "Feels like they are everywhere," John chuckled to himself during the pregame activities. The rest of the Nighthawks were ready. Thompson's pregame talk was interrupted by WGN, who wanted to air segments of the game. This juiced up the Nighthawks, knowing they'd be shown on television. When the camera focused on John, everyone took notice. John thanked the heavens and then his parents. He also thanked Coach Thompson. When asked the question, "How's the speed?" John sighed and with a broad smile commented, "We'll see." Harold, who happened to be in his McDugal office in downtown Chicago watching it on television, laughed heartily at the comments from his son. The news team thanked everyone and quickly left, hoping to catch the Razorblades. Larry knew his turn was coming, so he let it burn inside. The teams were ordered on to the field. Starting at linebacker for the Nighthawks were Williams, Myers, and Luwinski. Luwinski was a German who at fifteen qualified for

Wilburton. His lack of understanding the English language crippled him in some aspects, but he adapted quickly. His ability to read the field would help at the strong side position.

His near six-foot frame and 160 pounds wouldn't hurt either.

The sinister hitting Williams would be in the middle. Myers, the big softy, would be at the weak side, but his nose for the ball made him special. The crowd was excited. Top-notch high school referees would officiate. After the coin toss, it was decided Wilburton would kick off. This was where Alvin flourished, kicking the ball. A good kick that squiggled out of bounds at the fifteen-yard line of the Razorblades, which set things up. The Cotton Razorblades were ready. The Razorblade Coach, Andy Page, who at fifty two had previously coached high school football for five years had his boys fine-tuned. The sixty-thousand-dollar-a-year pay was too much for Page to turn down. Page, a former Canadian Football League running back, loved the offensive aspect of football. Not having a quick tailback, Page had to work with what he had. Tom Wilson, the Razorblade quarterback, glanced over at Coach Page before signaling the center to snap the ball. Page, who was balding and stood five foot nine and was slender except for the potbelly, winked at Wilson with his left eye. This gave Wilson, thirteen, the preseason choice for all league quarterback, a chance to test his rifle of an arm. His signal call of "one thirty seven" three times, and then the center would snap the ball after the fourth "hut." This was all done in under five seconds. The defensive front line for Wilburton were scrappy, which helped make up for their lack of height. The tallest, Eric Turner, who weighed a hefty 180 pounds was okay, but his five-foot-six frame made it difficult to go over the top on pass rush. For that matter, none of the kids in the trenches were what Gus looked for in his defensive tackles. Wilburton's hopes lay with its linebacker core.

Wilson grabbed the ball from the big center, Jason Tillman, who stood at least five eight and weighed a hefty 220 pounds. Tillman drove forward simultaneously. Wilson, now in the pocket, threw sixty yards down field, incomplete. He threw ten yards beyond his nearest receiver. With the power of Wilson's arm, Thompson sent in his reserve defensive back. Al Jones, who brought in the message, pass rushed the next three series. With the message of the pass rush, Larry felt the adrenaline flowing. As Wilson received the ball from the center, he quickly, on the strong side, lofted the ball to his fullback, Nathan Holmes, who at fourteen didn't have John's speed; but at 210 pounds, Holmes made tackling him interesting. Holmes quickly got behind the two pulling guards on the rush play. Larry read the play, busted through the offensive tackles, and gave Holmes all of his right-shoulder pad. Holmes, coiling for the blow, exploded on Greydog. Alvin Myers went low on Holmes, who managed a gain of two. The large audience showed its appreciation by letting out a large, "Ooooh!" Gus loved it; he jubilantly screamed, "Stay with it, Williams, way to help out Myers!"

Cheerleaders wouldn't be used this season to the dismay of all the players. The summer weather of early August showed. By the middle of the third quarter, there was still no score. Cade, who fumbled twice with Wilburton at the goal line, sat out most of the second quarter.

With the weather cooling down, Coach Thompson decided to put John back in. Not liking to use his players both ways, Thompson had to stretch his talent. Wilburton had possession at their own thirty. Harmen watched Cade trot into the huddle. John relayed from Coach Thompson, "Three rushes." John, now relaxed, felt ready. John knew of three Razorblade players who were sitting this play out. The right side was weak. "Five fifty-two, five fifty-two, hut hut, hike!" Harmen faked a short pass as he looked over at the stingy Razorblade defense, then lofted the ball to his right to Cade. John, already churning to the right, caught the ball and tucked it into his right cradle. In full stride, John pushed himself to the limit. He beat everyone to the corner. *If I can make it to the edge of the field without slipping,* John thought as he gulped in air; he didn't slip.

With cameras rolling, WGN taped the whole segment of John's gallop. John, now at the fifty, pushed himself to the limit. He was now at least ten yards ahead of the closest defender. The crowd stood; the noise was deafening. It washed over John like a wave; he sprinted harder. Number 30 was going to be something special. Seventy-yard screen play touchdown! Nighthawks led; when Myers kicked the extra point, the score read 7-0, Nighthawks. Coach Thompson yelled, "Damn, fine run, son, way to hang onto the ball!" as John trotted to the sidelines with teammates along. Larry, his eyes slits, nodded his head; John ignored him. Thompson could see the ice between the two. He then yelled, "Get in there special team, get into their ass!" Razorblades, after a strong kick, took it at the twenty-five yard line. When Razorblade quarterback Wilson was in the pocket, Luwinski blindsided him; Wilson coughed up the football. Larry, seizing the opportunity, quickly tracked the ball down. He then growled as he gathered the ball up and sprinted with the grace of a gazelle toward the end zone.

To the delight of the crowd, Larry gave a glimpse of the instinct Gus Thompson put into his kids. The spectators cheered wildly for the Nighthawks. When the game ended, the score read, "Wilburton 13, Northside 0." John went over to mingle with his associates from his neighborhood. Larry, with permission from Coach Thompson, showered and left early. The Nighthawks would seem to be the team to beat at this stage in the season. School officials were almost slobbering at the mouth, realizing the potential impact of the new middle school competition.

That night at home, Barbara, now feeling something different about her only son, wanted more babies. "Go ahead and shower, Johnny. Daddy will be home shortly, and I want you to be clean for dinner."

"Okay, Mom," John said smiling at Barbara as he headed for the deluxe bathroom. Harold was exhausted after a day at the office. Still he was beaming as he walked into the doorway of the family living room. He headed for his lover, he then patted her on the rump, and, as Barbara turned around, Harold put his arms around her and spoke to his sweetheart, "Hello, dear."

"Hi, honey," Barbara joyfully responded as she gave Harold a deep and tender kiss. John had just finished dressing himself, wearing his favorite summer attire, one of the cutoff Adidas jumpsuits. John owned six pairs of the jumpsuit, all of them in different colors. Harold stood and observed his son. John, not knowing what else to do, blushed. "Ah, come on, Dad, it's only a game."

"I know, son, but you're a rare find, and I appreciate being your father." John, not knowing what else to say, waved his hand in Harold's direction and said, "Thanks, Dad."

"You're welcome, son." Harold, starved, looked at his wife. "So, dear," he asked in his lover-boy tone with arms wrapped around Barbara, "what's the plan for dinner tonight?"

"I thought we'd order two large pizzas with fried chicken," Barbara lovingly replied. Harold happily responded in his pet name for Barbara, "Bee, you sure love chicken."

"Well, honey, I'd be fibbing if I said I didn't," Barbara proudly boasted. Harold let out his heckling sound. He remembered his wife and her stories of her childhood back in Oklahoma very well. But meeting his sweetheart during a vacation in Australia was a blessing in disguise. They both felt the attraction, and neither was afraid to fulfill their curiosity for each other. "What do you say, son, pizza and fried chicken?"

"Love some, Dad." John's mouth began to water. "I sure do feel bad about those fumbles. Gee, Dad, did you ever play football?" Harold looked away as he said, "No, son. I'm not as brave as you are." Barbara, sensing Harold getting uncomfortable, changed the subject by asking, "Soft drinks anyone?" Harold nodded then looked over at John. "How about you, son, would you like a soft drink?"

"Milk for me, Dad." Seeing that Barbara was already out of sight and into the kitchen, Harold yelled, "Milk for John!" Hours later, the family, when finished eating, had left nothing from the delivered food. John excused himself from the table. "I'm going to see Carolyn, is it all right, Mom and Dad?"

Barbara answered, "Be back before 10:00 p.m., okay, John?" John looked over at Barbara as he shot out, "Sure thing, Mom."

"She means it, son, so keep your word."

"I will, Dad." The customary peck on the cheek to Mom and John was out of the apartment and into the elevator. Once downstairs, John dialed Carolyn's number. Mr. Jones answered, "Hello."

"Hello, Mr. Jones, this is John. Is Carolyn in?" Mr. Jones's voice grew enthusiastic.

"Hi, John, hey, you did great, son, I saw you on the news." John felt mildly embarrassed yet proud. "Thanks, Mr. Jones, I appreciate it."

"Hold on a second, I'll go fetch Carolyn."

"Thanks."

"Hello." Her voice made his heart beat fast as always.

"Hey, Carolyn, so nice to hear your voice."

"You coming over, John?"

"Yes."

Carolyn sounded pleased as she asked, "Want Dad to come pick you up?" John had thought about this already. "No, I'll walk the four blocks to walk off some of my stiffness." She chuckled. "You mean you're stiff? You didn't play much except when you blew right past the whole team."

"I only took what they gave me, Ms. Jones."

Carolyn was feeling dreamy. "Sure, John, see you when you get here, okay?"

"Good-bye, till then, my friend."

Carolyn loved John's poetry; it gave her goose pimples. "Okay, John, bye."

To John, over to Carolyn's in the airish evening was a welcome feeling when the sun wasn't at its peak. "It's 7:43 p.m.," John said as he looked at his watch. "I should have taken the ride. Oh well, I do need to loosen up my hamstrings. They've been tightening up on me." It was totally different when walking than when using transportation. "Man! This gives me the willies." John walked quickly. Even though there were people out at this hour, John still didn't feel safe. John began mentally perceiving his fantasy of taking the streets of America back. "I kind of feel like a fool. I'm sure that could never happen, but darn, there are some people out there who would love for law and order to be the force." Carolyn had the door open. Her family, knowing the Cades well, welcomed John Cade. The home, a luxuriously built job, was at least a five-hundred-thousand-dollar home; this always reminded John that success was a must in his life. Mrs. Sandra Jones was originally from St. Paul, Minnesota, who at thirty-nine felt as young as a teenager. Her diet, as well as her training routine, kept Sandy fit and trim. Except for the few wrinkles around the eyes and the neck area, Sandra didn't look a day over twenty-five. The hourglass figure and the way Sandy kept her hair in a pony tail didn't hurt her youthful appearance either. Through her almond-shaped eyes, John could see where Carolyn received her good looks. Sandy, who at five ten, possessed blonde hair, made one feel she modeled for a living; yet Sandy loved her husband's role as a breadwinner so much that she decided to become a homemaker, which suited Dalton just fine. The harsh world of the clothing business didn't suit well with Dalton even though his wife earned a decent living selling intimate apparel for women. Dalton's ability as a mystery writer more than provided for his two sweethearts. Dalton, a tall man, stood six foot six and carried over 250 pounds of flesh, which gave him an intimidating presence. His curly black hair sat well atop of his balding head. His soft handsomely arranged facial features always reminded one of brilliance.

John, once in Carolyn's room with her parent's permission, openly studied Carolyn. John reached for Carolyn; somehow all the excitement of tackle football left him aroused. "Don't make me scream, Mr. Jekyll." This was Carolyn's nickname for the seemingly innocent-acting John. "One day, someone is going to find you out, and then what would you do?" Carolyn teased.

"I'll blame you, Carolyn. I'll say, 'Carolyn started me, and I can't stop.'" John lived for these moments. Suddenly, remembering earlier in the day, Carolyn stiffened and said, "Oh, John, did you know that guy Larry saw where we lived?" Alarmed, John asked, "Did he see you, Carolyn?"

"I'm not sure if he recognized me, okay?" Carolyn began to tremble and then went on, "But last Monday, while I was standing in the driveway, he and another black guy passed by on bicycles."

John tensed, then he added, "Maybe he didn't recognize you. Anyway, don't worry about it, Carolyn, he's not stupid."

Relaxing a little, Carolyn added, "Let's hope so."

Larry had spoken to three members of the Nighthawks, all of whom were black. Todd Holmes, Edbert Hillman, and Cornell Peal. Larry realized that if he could seduce these three young Negroes, it probably meant fifty or sixty men within the next month. All came from middle-class black families, yet they wanted to identify with the brothers. As the four men stood on 103rd patiently waiting, Arthur finally showed up. The powerful-sounding dual exhaust explained itself as Lisa dropped Arthur off and pulled back into traffic. Excited now, Larry spoke first, "Hey, Arthur X, these three are here to view a sample of our newly formed club."

"Great," Arthur X said and then shook hands with the three men. As he unlocked the door of the warehouse, he ushered everyone inside. Arthur began explaining to the four youths his dreams for, as he called it, freedom. Then Arthur tested the youth, he sang out, "All praise to revolt!" Arthur then went on, "See, brothers, we can do it. All we need is your cooperation, the more people, my young warriors, the stronger the unity." Arthur really had the youth beaming. "You see those barrel, brothers? They're especially designed to train men how to use rifles."

"You for real man!" Cornell popped out. Cornell, who played wide receiver, had the postpuberty voice and was ready for action. At five foot six and solid, Cornell weighed a svelte 128 pounds. The African features stood out on Cornell. The black skin, also the sharp nose due to the Indian heritage, was a sharp contrast to the otherwise rough-featured thirteen-year-old. The athletic body of Cornell made him a standout. Next to Cade, Cornell ran the fastest time on the Nighthawks.

"Yes, I'm for real, brothers." While the four observed the specially designed targets, Arthur went to a large locked metal container in the warehouse. He came out carrying two AK-47 assault rifles. Edbert let out a smooth whistle. "Man, let me hold one of them muthas."

Arthur X answered, "I will, babe, just take your time, they're not loaded." Edbert, the reserve quarterback, stood a shade under six feet and weighed a soft 150 pounds. Edbert figured he'd never start over Orosco but backup was cool with him. Not a very handsome fellow and the tragedy of having acne didn't help matters much, but with the silver tongue, Edbert could talk his way through most situations. Coming from an educated family, Edbert knew better than to join a gang. He'd always say, "Nigger, my age in a gang will either be in the pen or dead." But now, Edbert realized you have to have protection on these streets. Todd Holmes, a cousin to the Razorblades' Nathan Holmes, was the only legitimate high schooler on the Nighthawks squad. His solid 150 pounds earned him a spot on the offensive line. His five-foot-four frame earned him the nickname Stubby. The short coarse hair, the high chubby cheekbones, Todd looked like a short and darkened Buddha. After twenty minutes of Arthur showing the young men the different positions of firing, he decided to call it a night. "Call me, Greydog!"

"I will, X, all praise to revolt!" Larry yelled.

"All praise to revolt," Arthur sang back and gave up the salute. Arthur then escorted the four youths outside; he then went back inside the building to make sure it was secure. Larry, getting an idea, insisted on going by the Jones home. "Now I know where Cade's bitch lives, and if I catch up to him, I can get in his ass!" Larry was beside himself with fury. Edbert, hearing of Larry's escapade with John, was all too eager to try Cade. Edbert paused before he spoke and then said, "He think he's tough shit anyway, don't he, Greydog?" Edbert couldn't wait to get that statement out. Larry looked at the scarred face of Edbert, then he finally got out, "He sure do, Ed, but I have news for him, if we catch up to him. I know for sure he's over that fine-ass bitch's house!" Edbert, concerned now, spoke out, "What if five O show up dog?" Larry was hitting a fist in his palm. "Man, we will be out of the way before the man show up," Larry slang out. Arthur, now having the building secured, interrupted the four young men. "What's up, fellas, what are you boys plottin'?" he said in a laid-back manner.

Greydog barked out, "Going for Cade, man!" Arthur, not objecting but concerned, voiced his opinion, "You young tomcats, be careful." Cornell, who'd been quiet most of the evening, spoke up, "I just hope nothing happens to us being on the Nighthawks." Everyone fell silent. Todd, taking advantage of the situation, ran in the opposite direction. Ignoring Todd,

Arthur X broke the silence, "Get out of here before I turn you, young hoodlums, in myself."

"All praise to revolt." Larry closed the deal. As the three walked away from the now-training facility, they decided to try and locate a cab. After successfully hailing one of the few taxis in the vicinity, the three hunkered in for the long ride to the area of Lake Shore Drive. Larry, thinking of the prior cab, tried to keep a low profile. Cornell, in his ever deepening voice, managed to get out, "Pla-pla-play some music!" Larry touched Cornell on the knee and gave him the finger over his closed mouth, meaning, be easy. Cornell nodded. With traffic busy, the trip took longer than usual.

After seemingly hours, Larry now in the vicinity yelled, "Stop the cab! Stop the cab!" Larry was out and running before Al made a complete stop on East Oak Street. Larry believed he noticed Cade's form walking down the darkened street. "Hey, what's the freaking hurry? I need my sixty-eight bucks!" Al yelled in a slow Alabama drawl. Edbert, sensing trouble, drew out four twenties. "Take this my man, tip's on me." Al Jones at twenty-nine could no longer coach Little League basketball at the local YMCA for fondling girls; he was never one to turn down money. The scrubby full beard, the unkempt clothes, the oily skin. In Al's estimation, this kept away thieves. Through the chipped two front teeth, Al got out sarcastically, "Thanks, boy!" Edbert, usually up for a challenge, let the remark go. Edbert stepped proudly out of the cab. Cornell, already running in full stride, was on his way after Greydog and was out of Edbert's sight. The chilly sixty-degree weather after 9:00 p.m. was beautiful, with the breeze coming from the lake. Edbert, sensing this would be a long night, sighed and took to running. The homes were well kept and easy to look at. If it weren't for them running, Edbert wouldn't have minded sightseeing. The people mingling and hanging around didn't slow the two ahead of Edbert, so he continued to run. When Edbert finally caught up with the two, there was Cade, maybe twenty yards ahead, walking alone. Larry, twitching now as he caught his breath, yelled, "Hey, bitch called Cade, I want your ass!" With the window open in her room, Carolyn swore she heard a familiar voice. "Larry!" She rushed downstairs to get her father.

John, who had a gut feeling this evening would be something he would regret, turned around. John thought, *Not one but three people, Edbert too.* John knew Cornell would run, but Edbert had a chip on his shoulder about whites anyway. John yelled, "What do you want, Williams!" Greydog approached John. "Look, you white muthasucker, this is for you." Larry drew back, swung, and hit John in the middle of the face. John, now with tears streaming from the force of the blow, didn't wince. "Damn you, nigger!" Being taught not to use racial epithets, but John couldn't help it. He then added, "I'll kill you." The martial arts John was taught in elementary school kept him from losing his head. Edbert then circled around John and tried to grab him. Edbert received an elbow to the midsection; he went down. Cade, sensing the moment, stomped Edbert on the stomach. Edbert screamed, but only air came out. Larry stepped over his fallen comrade and took three violent right-handed haymakers that missed. John, in a defensive stance, tried a frontal kick. Larry blocked it.

A crowd was beginning to form. Dalton ran up and got in the middle of the crowd. His sheer size enabled Dalton to ram right through the thirty or so spectators who had formed a semicircle around the combatants. Dalton, finally getting close enough to John, grabbed him and walked back toward the Jones's home with his arm around John. No one dared stop the semigiant; a policeman showed up. Officer Stanton, who enjoyed this area during his beat, wasn't too thrilled to see three black youths who obviously weren't from the area.

At five foot seven, and well over two hundred pounds of muscle, Stanton had little trouble breaking up the crowd. "All right, all right, people, let's get back to our homes. There's no need to have me call for reinforcements." All the *damns* and other negative comments reassured Stanton that the civilians were complying with his orders. Stanton, sensing Dalton's commanding presence and also the young white kid he had a protective arm around with the bleeding nose, stepped up to Dalton. "Excuse me, sir, what seems to be the trouble here?" Dalton sized up the pint-sized gorilla with the close-cropped hair and penetrating eyes. His immaculate appearance, along with his boyish grinning face, kept Dalton from losing his already-boiling temper. "Well, Officer, five minutes sooner and my future son-in-law wouldn't have a sore nose." Larry and company used the moment to start heading in the opposite direction. "I'm sorry, sir," Stanton feigned sincerity, "but if you want to file a complaint—" John abruptly ended that idea by yelling out, "We don't want to file a complaint, Officer!" Happy now, Stanton politely said, "Now, you see there's nothing to worry about, Mr . . . . ?" Stanton waited for a reply, finally Dalton exhaled and blew out, "The name is Jones, Officer." Dalton, not knowing what else to do, thanked the officer and escorted John toward his home.

As Dalton and John left the scene, Officer George Stanton tried to find out from the crowd who was the perpetrator; he received little response. Finally, he threw up his hands and left the scene. Larry, leading the trio away from the scene, started walking. "Okay, Ed and Co"—his nickname for Cornell—"let's stop this running," Larry said while catching his breath. "We'll bring too much attention in a neighborhood like this."

"You're right, man," Edbert said, then he began to feel the led in his legs. He wanted to lie down on one of the manicured lawns in the area, but he pushed himself. Cornell spoke out. "I have money, shit, let's get a damn cab and go back to South Side, man."

"My thoughts exactly," Larry commented. Tired now, he wanted to sleep, but the excitement of busting Cade in the face had juiced him up. "When we get out of this neighborhood, I'm leaving that damn white boy alone, man, screw this shit," Cornell said between clenched teeth. He couldn't believe he had agreed to something so insane. Larry scolded his friend, "Aw, nigger, you can't get scared of little shit like this. Damn, Co, remember the rifles boy? It's going to get a lot tougher than this one day." Larry felt for his protégé. Edbert noticed a checker and began yelling for it. "Taxi, taxi!" The three entered the cab gratefully. For now, they were spared the pain of an arrest.

CHAPTER 4
THE MOMENT

August 6, 1993, school would start the following Monday. Coach Thompson, after his final preseason practice, had all the Nighthawks in full gear lined up. "Now listen up, girls, after our scrimmage against the Razorblades, a couple of my men tried to rearrange my running back's face. Now, after an angry fax from my friend, Mr. Harold Cade, threatening legal action for some Nighthawks cracking a bone in little Johnny's nose, I had no other recourse but to tell Mr. Cade I would handle the situation!" Gus handed John his office key. "John, bring those two boxes stacked against the rear wall in my office." It took John twenty minutes to walk all the way across campus and haul the four-foot long, one-foot high boxes back to the football field. "Here, Coach." John let the lightweight load fall to the earth. John was curious as to what the boxes contained. "Good, son," Gus said. "Now open them." As John opened the boxes, the team whistled. Gus, seizing the moment, spoke out, "Now you three involved, you either take your punishment or walk away from my team forever." No one moved. Larry wanted to run, but his life hinged on this project. Thompson then ordered Williams, Hillman, and Peal to strip to the waist. He then ordered each Nighthawk to pick up a hose and form a line, seventeen players, long odd man on right side. Cornell, tears streaming down his face, went first. The "thack, thack, thack" across the back couldn't conceal

Cornell's violent screams. He ran as fast as he could, but the viciousness of the blows were shattering to his central nervous system. As Peal neared the end of the line, Gus stood there, blocking the way. "Go back through, Peal!" The menacing looks he received from the Nighthawks almost caused Cornell to just give up, but knowing there was nothing out there without football, Cornell screamed, covered his face, and powered his way through the rubber hoses.

Todd snickered as he whacked Cornell across the back. The tongue-lashing he received from the trio for running the other night and the disbarment from the gang made Cornell relish being able to get revenge. Larry walked through. The loudness of rubber hitting flesh was evident. The pain was so great; Larry wanted to lie down and curl up, but he knew one day, the glory would be his, so he went ahead and took the punishment. The position the field was in concealed it from outside viewing. The large six-foot-high brick fence surrounding the back of the school kept everything viewable from inside only. Edbert refused to go through. Gus then yelled, "Get him!" The Nighthawks then mercilessly beat Edbert. Two minutes of Edbert lying on the ground squirming and crying like a woman sickened Coach. Thompson finally ordered everyone to quit beating Edbert.

He then commanded the team to hit the showers. Everyone then piled the hoses in the boxes and prepared to end practice. Thompson then ordered the fight song in unison. "Fight Nighthawks fight, when we hit there will be fright, win or lose we have the right, to be Nighthawks! ALL RIGHT!" After the song, Thompson suggested that the three that took the beatings stay put. Gus was going to make sure his message got across. Thompson let the rest of the team get away from earshot. "Hey, listen, you three," Thompson was sympathetic, "I'd have loved to forget the whole episode between yourselves and Cade, yet you left me no choice." Now Gus faced Williams. "Now, look, Larry, I'm just about at the end of my rope with you, son." Larry, angry now, said nothing, but he glared right back into Coach's eyes. "One more incident, son," Thompson put both hands on Larry's shoulders then added, "and I'll let the law have you. You got that?"

The emphatic tone Gus used forced Larry to nod his head weakly in agreement, yet the tears hanging on the edge wouldn't fall. Thompson, sensing his point was well taken, ordered the three to wait outside the locker room until everyone else finished up for the day. As Thompson left the trio, Edbert was the first to speak. Through convulsions, Edbert managed to stutter out, "I-I-I could kill Coach, letting this shit happen." Larry, the pain evident, let the statement soak in. Cornell was rubbing some of the large welts on his arm. He ignored the rest of his anatomy, which stung as if ants were biting at raw skin. He couldn't stop trembling. After what seemed like hours, Larry stood up. He looked in to the locker room. They had been sitting there over two hours. Larry, sensing his authority, harshly but softly urged his soldiers to hit the showers. This was going to be a long evening.

Carolyn, who stopped meeting John after practice at the school gate, was thrilled to see John in such good spirits as she walked through the front door of the Cade residence. She purposely ignored his swollen face. "Why you feeling so good, Johnny?" Barbara, knowing this was Carolyn's fun time with her son, announced that she was going into the kitchen for some snacks. Barbara was all too thrilled that Coach would start bringing John home from practice, especially with these little incidents. Barbara, from the look on John's face, knew all too well that Harold's plan about punishment worked.

John, sensing Carolyn's mood was cheerful, gave her a tight hug. "I feel good because school starts Monday, and the arduous task of getting educated is right in front of me."

Carolyn smiled then added, "Oh, John, you're such a child. You mentioned before that you hated education on several occasions." John, stammering because of Carolyn's remarkable memory, admitted, "I used to, but now that football is going so well, I've changed my tune." He then playfully winked at his girl. Carolyn laughed a loud childish soprano "hahaha", which made her blush. John's smile at her embarrassment caused Carolyn to roll her eyes. As her head was turning to either side, she noticed the perfect view of the lake in the Cade home. The family photos were sparse yet full of family history. Carolyn loved looking over the lake at the height of the apartment. The glitter of sun hitting the water was magnificent. With this visit to the Cade home, Carolyn thought she'd be nosy. "John, now this person right there on the wall, that looks like you."

"Oh, that's Grandpa, Will Cade." John felt like a museum historian. "You see, Carolyn, over a century ago, this man, my grandfather, was an educated Indian. He thrived on his good looks." Carolyn burst out with laughter and after a few moments of the insanity blurted out, "Now come on, Cade, isn't that a little prejudice?" John at full tilt continued, "Will also was a banker who earned over two million dollars in his lifetime. He also held his own bear trapping, as you can see," John pointed to the bearskin rug on the floor, "and he was tough enough to legally walk the streets with a Caucasian woman." Carolyn was quiet and deeply listening to John. Finally, she interrupted, "John, you think one day you and I could look this up on the Internet or do some research at the library?"

John one step ahead of Carolyn, mentioned, "Dad purchased a book some twenty years ago about famous Apache warriors, and my grandfather, Will, has an article written in it about him."

Excited, Carolyn asked, "When can I see it, John?" Before John could answer, Barbara came back into the living room. "Anyone for snacks?" This seemed to be a welcome relief for the two, who immediately dove into the celery and peanut butter with crackers and cheese.

Harold, still steaming over traffic, lightly opened the door; he couldn't sneak in. "Hello, my sweetness," Barbara said as she rushed over to give her hubby a sensual peck on the cheek. "Hey, I did nothing," Harold was feigning his innocent act. Barbara, feeling sheepish, said it anyway, "Oh yes, you did." The two, now laughing, embraced.

Harold noticed Carolyn, then he spoke to her, "Well, hello, Carolyn, I didn't see you."

"Hi, Mr. Cade." Carolyn then waved. Harold, not wanting to upset Carolyn, asked his son, "How did practice go, son? Pretty rough?" John, now realizing Harold's ploy was not to alarm Carolyn, responded, "It went well as usual, Dad, until the end of practice, then things got tough." This intrigued Carolyn, who innocently asked, "How?" John, now on a hook, unhooked himself. "Well, you could say there was a lot of regret for some of the players." After the laughter ceased, Carolyn, still not understanding, brushed it off as one of those days. Harold was famished after a hard day at work; he stopped chuckling long enough to ask, "What's for dinner?" Barbara nodded at Carolyn. Carolyn, quickly with her rehearsed line proudly proclaimed, "We are all cordially invited to the Jones residence for a feast, courtesy of Sandra Jones."

"Now, that's what I call good timing." Harold couldn't believe his good fortune. "Now let's get going."

The three Nighthawks, beaten, burning, and angry, finally made it to Wilma's run-down apartment. They had spent the major part of the evening at Seal's playing pool and forgetting their worries through the power of suds. Larry, now back to the present, wouldn't let go; the thoughts roared through him. "Cade is mine, but I can't lay hold of his ass now or I will never leave this dump." Collecting his thoughts, Larry was slow to speak. He even took time to notice his two sidekicks. Then Greydog spoke, "Hey, you two, I know both of you are mad, but let's drop this shit and deal with our goal man, Brotherhood of the Oppressed, damned all this other shit!" Peal and Hillman, now semidrunk, yelled, "All praise to revolt!" Crying now, the three men embraced. Larry, realizing the leadership bestowed upon him, made a statement concerning Cade. "Let's drop the petty shit with Cade, play ball, and get with X, man." Edbert, the liquor easing, with the welts almost invisible, spoke up, "You know, Greydog, it's all to be damned if I was going home with all those welts on my ass! My mom would have a fit." The three chuckled. Cornell, still thinking of that punk-ass Todd, spoke through fits of laughter, "Damn, Todd got clean away this time, but I won't forget his ass!" The door suddenly opened, it was Wilma. "You, boys, okay out there?"

"Yes, Grandma, we'll be in in a second, okay?" Larry reassured Wilma.

"Well, your two friends—people have been calling here for them." Sensing the time, Wilma let the three men know it. "It's after ten at night, should be in bed."

"Okay, Mom," Larry, feeling his love for Wilma, the only positive adult in his home life right now, promised he'd be right in.

After the scintillating cry of "all praise to revolt," Larry retrieved his comrades' bicycles. "You two be easy, school is on Monday, and we have some recruiting to do." Larry eyed his troops. They both nodded and, in unison, mounted their bicycles and headed toward their respective homes. Wilma made one final check on Larry. "Larry!"

"I'm coming, Mom." Once inside the apartment, Larry eyed the familiar belongings of his grandmother. The small guest room and the dingy white paint with chips missing reminded Larry of his toddler years when he imagined the chips were faces. The old sagging couch, the small color television set. He and Wilma used to spend so much time together watching television. The creaky wooden floor specially put in by Wilma years ago was in need of repair, and this reminded Larry, *One day, I'm going to leave Momma.* Larry then went over and tightly hugged his (as he would say) mother. Wilma, giving Larry more space because of puberty, was surprised at the boy's sudden surge of affection, but she hugged him back anyway. "Ouch, ouch." Shocked, Wilma hurriedly asked, "What's wrong, boy! Is it that football you are playing?"

Larry feebly managed a "yes, grandma" as he winced in pain.

"Take of your shirt and let me see," Wilma sternly asked.

"Ahh, Grandma." Larry, too embarrassed, wouldn't comply.

Again, Wilma roughly repeated, "Now don't sass me, boy! Take off your shirt." As Larry slowly pulled his stylish blue-gray polo shirt over his head, Wilma whistled, "Boy, whoever got hold of you wasn't playing. That's not football. What have you been doing, boy?" Wilma looked at Larry concerned. "Just some trouble I got into, Mom, I'll be all right." Larry faked a smile. Wilma, realizing trouble was the only thing in life for poor people, shrugged her shoulders. She went into the small but clean restroom and came out with some Vaseline. She then made Larry lie facedown on the couch and rubbed some of the Vaseline onto the wounds covering Larry's back. "Keep you from getting too dry," Wilma said. After rubbing Larry down, Wilma urged Larry to get some sleep; life was waiting for him.

Gus woke up from his evening nap. He looked at the clock on the wall in his basement, which years ago he turned into a den; it was 10:52 p.m. The quart of Jack Daniel's lay on the floor; only a corner of the bottle contained liquid. The telephone rang, and after the third ring, the answering machine took over. Gus heard a familiar voice; it was Harold Cade's. "Hello, Mr. Thompson, sorry I called so late, but I had to say this, thanks for the help, sleep tight, Gus." Harold hung up. Gus, pretty ripped up on the liquor now, finally managed to set himself straight upon the couch. Harold's suggestion was crude, but it seemed to affect the three young men drastically. Gus now wondered, *Could I face these youth during the next practice? If they turn me in, I'll never coach again, that's for sure.* Gus, who always was the big man wherever he went, started reminiscing about the past.

After four strong years as an offensive tackle for the University of Nebraska, Gus was a cinch to go pro. Not once in his collegiate career did any defensive linemen or linebacker get past him. Then the unthinkable happened. The Fiesta Bowl in 1957. In the third quarter of the game, with Nebraska holding on to a thirteen-point lead, Gus stood up Harold Faulkner on a third down play. Faulkner, at the time, was one of the best defensive linemen in the college ranks. Gus remembered it well.

Another player from the opposing side, Sandle Wilson, illegally slammed into the front of both Gus's knees. The memory sobered Gus. Both legs broke backward, the feeling of bone breaking, the intense pain, the screaming. Gus had to hang on to Faulkner, who had to gently let Gus go forward and lay facedown. Six years of surgery. Gus felt lucky to walk normally, yet there would not be any great strength flowing through those knees. Professional sports was out of the question. That's when the phone calls started coming, speaking engagements, jobs. Gus earned a substantial amount of money over the years, which he invested wisely. Never marrying left Thompson with ample time to drink away his sorrow. Williams popped into the memory of Gus. "Boy, that kid reminds me of a miniature Faulkner, but only Williams is black." Gus felt he respected the blacks more than what was required by society, yet you had to be tough on them, especially the youth of poverty. They just didn't respond well to kindness.

Still mentally visualizing his past, Gus probed until his memory went to the Bears. Gus was next in line for the vacancy at Head Coach. Fifteen years of service, then that stupid rookie fullback refused to respect the authority of Thompson. Gus, always the outspoken one, really tore into the rookie. The word *nigger* was used several times. During the questioning, several key witnesses who happened to hear the tongue-lashing testified against Thompson. The Bears organization, although devastated, had no choice but to release Thompson, who felt cheated but packed his bags and left the team. Still today, the organization did anything in its awesome power in Chicago to honor one of its own. Gus spotted the touch of the burning liquid. He opened the bottle, tilted it upward toward the sky, and braced himself for the famous taste of straight liquor going down.

CHAPTER 5
THE WAREHOUSE

The winter would be brutal this year in Chicago. The middle of November weather was an immediate reminder of the things to come. The temperature, which constantly hovered around the forties during the day and with lows in the thirties, kept the Windy City natives bundled up. Not to mention the wind. The Nighthawks, always the hard workers, didn't live up to expectations this year. Cade was the top rusher in the league, yet his fumbles cost the team three vital contests that possibly cost them a spot at the league playoffs.

With a record of seven wins and five losses, third place would have to do this year. Coach Thompson was still pleased with his team's effort; he wouldn't show his disappointment at the hard-hitting team's underachieving status this year. After the last contest against the Eagles of Clintwood who came from the former Morgan Park, Thompson wanted one last lecture until next season. He kept his players out on the field. The school was just as spectacular as Wilburton but with smaller bleachers. During the contest, which the Eagles won twenty-one to fourteen, five hundred showed, which was the full capacity. "Now listen up, men." Thompson proudly surveyed his Nighthawks, then added, as he looked back and fourth at each man, holding an empty pipe he kept handy during each contest. "We've come along way, team, I know we didn't live up to the expectations of everyone, but we competed well. I'm proud of you, fellas, now go over and congratulate the Eagles, and remember to tell them we will be there in the playoffs next year."

The five hundred and dozen or so spectators slowly headed home. People were so thrilled at such an effort to save inner city youth by the State of Illinois that they didn't mind the twenty-dollar gate fee. As John left the showers, he packed his gear in the large hamper and instead of riding the team bus, he headed for the school gates. Through the throngs of people, he finally, after at least ten minutes of searching, saw the Cade and Jones family looking for him. After noticing John, they got together and headed to the cramped parking lot down the street from the school to Dalton's ever-ready slightly worn blue 1978 Chevy Suburban. Once inside the vehicle, everyone looked forward to the vehicle warming up so they could get some heat. Dalton, who demanded that Harold sit up front with him, spoke first. "You did well, John." Dalton then patted Harold on the knee. He then looked back at John and commented, "Seventy-eight yards on only thirteen carries, you took a beating, son, but you certainly get my vote as being proud of you."

"I second that," Harold shot back. John, feeling good about things, answered Dalton, "Yes, Mr. Jones, but did you see me in the third quarter when I slipped? I know I'd have gained another sixty yards and scored." Then John pouted. "Stinky weather." John was frustrated at the slippery field conditions of the Clintwood field. "Now, don't fret, son," Dalton consoled John, "you led the league in touchdowns with eleven, and you have next year to improve. Sky's the limit, John." He then said admirably, "Where on earth did you get that speed?"

Barbara couldn't help but speak up. "From me, of course." Everyone, including Barbara, really got a laugh from that one; poor Dalton almost lost his grip on the steering wheel. "Okay, Mom, I bet you got it from chasing all those chickens on the farm back in Oklahoma." John thought he'd put his two cents in the folly. Through laughter, Harold suggested to his son to take it easy on Dalton's sense of humor. Giggling at the whole scenario, John promised he'd stop.

After all the activity of football, John realized he was famished. He wanted something to eat. Barbara, seemingly reading her son's mind, pulled a cold meat sandwich out of her carry bag. "Thanks, Mom," a grateful John said as he accepted the sandwich. Always the finicky eater, John had to ask, "What kind of meat, Mom?"

"Your favorite, John, sliced pastrami with mustard." As John, who sat in the rear of the Suburban, greedily took the last bite of the quick meal, the group pulled into a nearby McDonald's. The aroma of fried beef quickly filled everyone's senses through the heating system, which seemed to relax the two close-knit families. "Drive in or go inside?" Dalton hurriedly asked, hoping to get a quick answer before he committed himself to a parking space. "Drive thru," Sandy and Carolyn sang in unison. "Drive thru it is." Dalton happily swung the Chevy in the long line of cars and then switched on the specially designed recircular air.

Larry had gathered at least one thousand signatures for the gang, but he hadn't shown Arthur yet; and Arthur, not knowing the total, was anxious to see young Greydog's effort, not to mention Hillman's and Peal's. Arthur would lie awake some nights daydreaming of the way young Holmes bolted away from the trio that last summer and just burst with laughter. Lisa would always get mad at him for waking her up, but remembering the fear on the boy's face, it was too much. Back in his present state of mind, Arthur viewed himself as the leader of the gang, yet Terran carried most of the weight. Arthur got out of bed and started thinking of the day's events. A meeting would be held at the warehouse today, Sunday. After the Nighthawks' last game for the season yesterday, Arthur felt it was a nobrainer for the youth of oppression to flow in. Larry couldn't get a hold of Arthur for a month and a half. He'd been involved in recruiting youth who needed protection in their life. With the efforts of Williams, Peal, and Hillman, they had at least eleven hundred signatures of young, naive, and mostly honest teenagers who were promised to be taught how to use firearms. The youth who signed up were of several nationalities and were all too eager to be gang members. Saturday night, Larry finally got Arthur X on the phone. "Damn, Arthur, I thought you meant business, man, I have a whole lot of names and let me tell you, they're ready!" Arthur, now excited, yelled over the phone in his deep baritone voice, "Look, young JoJo, I've been busy getting empty warehouses. I purchased four large ones in areas where they will not arouse suspicion." Larry, curious now, shot back at Arthur, "Hey, man, where you getting all this money?" Arthur calmed his friend, "Don't worry, little Joe, everything's taken care of. Anyway, I'll inform you later, all right?" X was careful not to lose sight of the prize. "Now, you round up your people and tell them to meet us at the warehouse on 103rd." Arthur had to ask, "How many people have you talked to?" Brimming with pride, Larry cheerfully answered, "Over a thousand."

    Arthur bristled, "Damn, fella, you've been busy. Boy, we will have to organize this group." Then quickly thinking, Arthur suggested to Larry to bring only those he wanted to share leadership with. Larry, now proud of his new responsibility, assured X that only leaders would come. "Fine, Williams, have your team at my warehouse on 103rd at ten thirty Sunday morning, all right?"

Larry answered his friend, "I'll be there, Arthur." The brutal thirty-two-degree cold shook Larry out of his slumber. "Damn, this is the one time of the year I'd like to live somewhere else." Wilma, hearing her grandson stirring in his room, knocked on the door and informed Larry breakfast was ready. "Okay, Ma." Larry managed to get out through his chattering teeth. The small white-colored bedroom, the one-dresser drawer set with a small mirror on top of it was the only real valuable piece of furniture Larry owned. He had gotten it from Wilma; it was JoJo's. Larry treasured it. Quickly putting on a T-shirt and blue jeans, Larry rushed in to the living room and then to the small furnace. "Cold, son?" Wilma would always chuckle at Larry's frustration with winter. "It's some eggs and hamburger patties waiting for you in the kitchen." "Thanks, Ma." Larry was forever grateful to his grandma. After eating, Larry washed up and checked the time. "Shit, seven fifty-seven. I have to get moving." Wilma, knowing Larry wouldn't, he never did, but she asked anyway, "You going to church, boy? Your daddy never liked it, maybe that's why he's where he's at." This angered Larry. "Don't talk like that, Ma! Daddy didn't need church." Wilma corrected her only grandchild. "Everybody needs God." She said it in a way that Larry knew she cared. "Sorry, okay, Ma." Larry said as he rubbed his foot on the worn brown carpet. "Don't worry, son, when God wants you, he will call you." Larry remembered to be silent; Grandma had spoken her piece. He then took the only phone in the apartment to his room but not before thanking Grandma for breakfast. Larry planned his strategy. "I'll call Peal and Hillman and tell them niggers to bring four people apiece."

"Hello," Ms. Andrea Thomas said as she answered her phone. She wondered who's calling at such an ungodly hour for a Sunday. "Hi, Ms. Thomas, is Edbert there?" Andrea, now recognizing Larry's voice, relaxed. "Just a minute, Larry, I'll fetch him for you." Andrea, living in Chicago all of her life, and had given birth to Edbert at the age of fifteen, couldn't help but to be attracted to the young Williams boy. A heavyset woman, Andrea knew all to well what being attracted to men would do. The short kinky Afro, the dark brown skin. Andrea favored a young Aunt Jermima, yet her sheer street-smarts landed her a very lucrative position downtown as an assistant legal aid officer. The 34,000-dollar-a-year job more than provided her and Edbert a nice condominium on Lower East Side. She didn't understand why Edbert chose Wilburton over one of the newer schools that were closer to home. Andrea always teased herself, "Maybe he's running as far from his sorry ass father as I am."

"Hello," Edbert, still groggy from sleep and cranky, angrily yelled, "who is it?"

"It's me, man, G-dog. Call Peal and both of you bring four of your toughest men."

"What's going on, Larry?" Edbert anxiously asked, his mood brightening.

"X wants us to meet him at the warehouse on 103rd." Larry made sure Edbert got the message. "Be there at 9:30 a.m. I'll meet you there, all right." Edbert excitedly answered, "Gotcha, Larry, see you." Edbert hung up the phone and begun dialing. Larry, relaxed now that he had contacted his people, went to the small laundry room in the rickety apartment and retrieved his ten-speed. That old Schwinn of his dad seemed to last forever. "Damn, my shit is on flat, I have to get some patches from Sharkey." Larry, always the conversationalist as well as the listener of his own garb, informed Grandma he'd be right back. "Going over to Sharkey's, Ma."

Wilma yelled back at Larry, "Okay, boy, and take your key, never know nowadays." Wilma's concern for safety never failed to impress Larry. Sharkey lived a couple of rows down from Larry's apartment, which made the walk in the cold bearable for Greydog. He walked quickly to Sharkey's apartment. As he knocked on the door, Larry felt odd. After seemingly knocking forever, Quenlin answered the door, "Who's out there?" Larry, recognizing the familiar voice, yelled, "It's me Larry." Finally, and through sobs, Quenlin opened the door and hugged her lover. "What's wrong, girl?" Larry asked, then he thought of Sharkey. "Where's my boy?" Quenlin didn't answer; she sobbed even more. Mr. Davidson came into the ragged room of the typical ghetto apartment, sparse furniture with a torn and dirty once-white carpet with paint chips missing on the white-colored walls, yet life held its own here.

A small high yellow man, Josh and Sharkey could have passed for brothers instead of father and son. Yet at fifty-two, he carried his Indian heritage well. Josh, who served two years in the army, still couldn't break the grips of poverty; wild living didn't help matters much either. Yet his will to survive kept him in an upbeat manner most of the time.

"Sit down, son." Josh motioned over to Larry. Josh then eased his frail frame on an old milk crate. "I would offer you breakfast, but I'm all out of food till I get my check next week." Larry ignored Josh and then, sensing the worst, finally got it out, "What happened?" Shocked, Quenlin, through clenched teeth, shot back, "You don't know!"

Larry, disturbed, softly said, "No."

Quenlin informed her man. "Sharkey and Juanita were murdered last night at a birthday party." Quenlin ran over to Mr. Davidson and cried, hiding her face on poor Josh so Larry wouldn't see the tears. Her convulsions hurt Josh; he could only put his arms around her. Greydog stood there motionless, no tears, but sheer anger boiled to the top of his head. Larry hadn't seen his buddy for over three weeks, and now he's dead. Instinctively, Larry yelled, "Who did it?" After minutes of silence, Josh tried to calm Larry down. "Does it matter, son? My boy's gone on to be with his mother. I don't want to see no more killings, and besides you have to go on, live boy, don't look back. He's dead, Larry." The somber, pathetic way Josh handled his only son's death brought more anger out of Larry. Again, he yelled, "Who did it?" Finally, Quenlin blurted out, "We think a group of white boys did it. All I know is that when I went to use the restroom, I heard a bunch of shots. They sounded like balloons bursting. I stayed on the toilet, and when I came out, everyone was yelling and hollering. Then I saw them just lying on the ground with blood everywhere." She then informed Larry, "Four other people were shot too, but Sharkey and Juanita were hit bad." Stunned, Larry let it soak in, the memories, the days of childhood. The stealing, the girls, teasing Grandma. The powers of manhood then began to take over. He sternly asked Quenlin, "How long have you been here, girl?" Quenlin, sensing Larry's suggestion, was shocked at the accusation. "I don't believe you think I—" she cut herself short. Josh quickly interrupted, "No, son, I wouldn't do that to you." Josh understood the mind of ghetto youth. "I'm sorry, Josh, I didn't know." Larry now felt foolish. Mr. Davidson composed himself. "What brings you around, Larry?"

"I need to borrow some patches for my bicycle." Larry really felt sheepish now. Josh kindly suggested that he would fetch them for Larry. As Josh retrieved the patches, Quenlin just sat there and stared menacingly at Larry. She angrily thought, *I can't believe he would think something like that.* Larry, on the other hand, had thousands of thoughts roaring through his mind, yet he knew he was on shaky ground with Quenlin. Josh reentered the small living room, then he turned to Larry. "Here's all the glue and patches my boy left, Larry, you go ahead and keep them." Then figuring this was the best time to say it, Josh informed Larry that he had some more of Sharkey's things to give Larry. Sad now at the impact of his friend being dead, Larry tearfully said to Josh that he'd be back to collect Sharkey's belongings because he had things to do. Larry embraced his best friend's dad. He then went over to Quenlin to try and comfort her; at first she tried to stiffen, yet with Larry's soothing words of, "Sorry, sweetheart," she finally gave in. "Don't worry, Q, I'll do something. They can't just do my boy like that." Then the tears came down. Larry cried silently as he held his lady for seemingly hours. Larry, after giving Quenlin and Josh a final good-bye, left the Davidson home and headed to his grandmother's apartment. After he fixed the flat, Larry put on his heavy green windbreaker with a light blue sweater underneath. The long johns and the two pairs of thick white socks would do for the chilly ride on his bicycle to the warehouse. "It's not as cold as it's going to get," Larry reminded himself of the icy cold outside. He then looked at the time. "Damn, nine thirty already this morning, have to get moving." By the time he made it to the warehouse on 103rd, Larry, even though it wasn't snowing now, was sweating profusely under his clothing. Yet the pain of losing Sharkey seemed to fuel Larry's desire to be there. The bitter cold numbed Greydog.

Inside the warehouse, Arthur X was busy talking to all the young men who had already arrived at the large building. He was surprised to see Caucasian youth there, yet he felt he could trust the young teenagers' choices in their recruiting efforts.

Larry pounded on the door. "Get that, Hillman!" Arthur ordered. "And don't open it until you recognize them, Hillman!" Hillman rushed to open the door, as he stood inside the locked warehouse Hillman yelled, "Who's there."

Larry sarcastically said, "It's Goldie Lox, now let me in. Shit, it's cold out here!" Relieved now, Hillman opened the large metal door of the warehouse, which was locked from the inside. "You're late, Williams, don't let it happen again. I don't have time to give away." Arthur felt he had to exercise authority now. "Sorry, X." After the apology, Larry began getting out of his gear. Arthur let Greydog get situated, then he began instructing his new recruits. "Now listen up, fellas, I know you men are tired of all the bull crap that's going on in the streets, for that matter so am I; but now, with Greydog's idea of you men forming a team for protection, we can change things." Arthur had the youth's full attention. He then asked everyone to follow him to the rear of the large warehouse. As the group formed around X again, he pointed to eleven fifty-gallon drums with black dots all over them. Everyone just stared at the barrels. "Just a minute, men. Peal, Hillman, come with me." As Peal and Hillman followed X to the large metal industrial boxes, which were locked, they were shocked at what they saw. "Damn!" Hillman sputtered, then he let out a respectful, "Whew." The boxes, in Hillman's estimation, contained at least one hundred rifles apiece. Arthur then ordered Peal and Hillman to give everyone rifles. As he watched the excited young men grab the empty weapons, Arthur smiled. He then thought to himself, *It's about time this shit is getting together.* Arthur then grabbed one of the illegal machine guns; he felt ready to lay down the law to his new recruits. "I know everyone is excited, men," the street slur of X stood out, "but listen close, boys, you are the future leaders of Brotherhood of the Oppressed." Arthur went on, "Now usually, I wouldn't have my men deal with guns, but the way things are going on the streets, you never know what's going to happen." X kept informing the youth, "Now you, white boys, are not exactly what you call oppressed, but you can help keep us informed on white people matters." Everyone let out an excited burst of laughter. "Silence!" Arthur wanted complete subjection. Then, with his rifle at port arms, Arthur beamed as he said, "Now, observe a master at his craft." The youth observed Arthur demonstrate various positions. "Remember these positions, boys, especially the kneeling and standing ones. You may need them one day. Take heed, wise ones." The young men seemed to enjoy handling the menacing-looking AK-47. Arthur, viewing the young warriors, began to dream of taking over a city. He began thinking of the youth's heart. *Damn, young fools don't know shit. They think it's a game, probably from all that television.* Arthur then realized that they would have to do for now. Arthur walked behind his men as they dry fired at the black dots on the barrels. He began giving tips and showing each member the numerous positions on how to correctly hold the arms of battle. Arthur began teaching the youth how to aim the weapons, "Keep the sights centered, men." Arthur helped Williams adjust to the standing position with the assault weapon. After an hour of target practice, Arthur sensing the youths were losing interest, called it a day. After the weapons were locked away, Arthur, not letting up, further instructed his people, "Now, men, being good with guns takes discipline. You need more than bullets and a good hiding place. Now discipline," X was careful so that the words soaked in, "can keep you alive, people." Arthur, showing extraordinary patience, had the youth form a single line. "I want you young men here today to be my leaders. Now I have a lot of work to do being that I'll be training all of you, but from what

I've seen today, the hard work will pay off." After the lectures, Arthur gave each man a number, and as he called the number, the men would yell their last names. Arthur went on, ignoring the cold as he spoke, "In the future, gentlemen, I'm going to give all of you keys to this building. Now, the day I give you to come, you are my leaders, so bring fifty different people twice a month to practice with the weapons." Arthur surveyed the youth to try and detect perpetrators; he felt he didn't have any. "How many of you are afraid of dying?" No one spoke. X, serious, silently spoke, "If anyone goes to the authorities, he will be eliminated. We may be caught here, but the snitch will die!" After the threat, Arthur yelled, "All praise to revolt!" The group yelled back in unison, "All praise to revolt!" Arthur, in full control now, gave further instructions. "I know some of you are big, strong middle-school football players, and you are in great shape; yet too be a soldier, you have to have unity. So I want you all to master one hundred sit-ups and push-ups at home daily. I will bring pull-up bars here later. I have the silent oath papers to fill out later. Remember, gentlemen, you are my leaders." Arthur gave everyone his business card. "I'll be here from 3:30 p.m. to 10:30 p.m. daily. Anytime you want to talk, call me. Dismissed."

As the excited youth exited the warehouse and headed to their respective destinations, Larry waited for everyone to leave and slowly went up to Arthur. "Can I speak with you, X?"

"Sure, Greydog. What can I do for young JoJo?" The sobs, the shakes, and the tears of Larry alarmed Arthur. He thought to himself, *Damn, I hope he's not punking out now, we're just getting started.* "What's wrong, Greydog?" Arthur patted Larry on the back to reassure him. Larry finally managed to get out, "My boy got killed last night, Arthur. Some white bastards did it!" Hearing the story, Arthur relaxed. He said to himself, *Damn, he scared me for a minute. I thought the boy was yellow.*

Arthur spoke to Larry, "Listen, son, people do die in this world, but I'm sorry about your boy. I heard about that, two young people were killed at a party on East Forty-Seventh Street. He shouldn't have been there; those damn crazy immigrants. Listen, Larry, we've come a long way." Arthur was looking deep into Larry's eyes as he spoke. "I'm not saying forget about your boy, but stay focused. I'll look into it for you." This reassured Larry for he knew when Arthur asked questions, he got answers. "Thanks, Arthur," the grateful Larry whispered. "Any time, now get moving." Arthur then patted Larry on the back and gave him a hug. "Call me in a week for instructions and getting the keys distributed." They both parted. Larry went and picked up his wet overcoat, took out the beat-up but dependable green, twenty-seven-inch bicycle, and headed out. Arthur surveyed the warehouse and then headed for the small office in the rear of the building. Terran observed everything from his tinted window and was pleased. As Arthur came into the office, Terran had a few instructions for him. "My friend," Terran spoke in his Middle Eastern accent, "what I observed from your so-called recruits disappoints me." Terran continued, "A man with your knowledge of life should know you need much tougher men." Arthur defended his troops. "Listen, T, these people will grow into great soldiers, and from what you explained to me so far, we won't see any real action for some time." Irritated at Arthur, but realizing Arthur was right, Terran still wasn't satisfied. "This is true, Mr. X, yet I think you should at least have tougher leaders."

Inquisitive now, Terran asked about the young man in tears. Arthur slowly explained the tragedy. "Perfect," Terran exclaimed, "find out who did it, Mr. X, and let's send a couple of your people; and as the Americans say, we can test their testicles." Laughing, Arthur corrected his savior, "That's balls,

T." They both doubled over from laughter at Terran's misuse of the statement. Back in his serious mode, Terran still insisted on at least tougher leaders. Arthur answered Terran, "I'll see what I can do, boss."

"Good, how well are you doing with cash, Mr. X, and are you having difficulties moving money?" Terran studied X carefully. Arthur didn't flinch but proudly added, "Don't worry, T, my lady can just about cover any amount. She's a lawyer, you know." Pleased at Arthur's obvious intelligence, Terran gave the war cry, "All praise to revolt, Mr. X."

"All praise to revolt, Terran." The two shook hands. Realizing the time, Arthur cut the celebration short. "I better get moving. My lady is waiting outside by now." Caution flooded Terran now. "Be careful, my friend." Terran saluted Arthur X who, after returning the salute, headed to the exit and into the cold weather, which was acting very erratic this year. Terran, alone now, made a phone call. Speaking in his native tongue after the opposite receiver had been picked up, Terran began talking. "Everything's going fine, Muhammad, the Americans seem to enjoy the rifles. The other shipload of weapons will have to stay put until more people come from my associate Mr. X. In the meantime, let's keep a low profile. We will give them at least, as the foolish Americans would say, a decade. Then America is ours! Praise our God!" Terran abruptly hung up the phone. As he exited the rear entrance, he looked at the empty warehouse, winked to himself, and headed for the rear of the building where his custom Mercedes was parked, waiting for him.

CHAPTER 6
CHAMPIONS

Gus, excited, couldn't stop yelling as he ran down the sidelines. "Go, John! Go, John!" This was Wilburton's big moment. After last year's debacle, the team put it all together and had a perfect season. A win today and they would be city champs. John, in full stride, could hear the roar of the crowd. The old Grant Park was renovated to form the school who had named themselves the Christopher Daredevils, after the great explorer Columbus. The beautiful view of the lake seemed minimal due to number 22; his great strides had everyone going crazy.

The Daredevils, the only other undefeated team in the Cactus League, proved to be formidable. They also possessed speed demons. George Halen, a scrawny defensive back with tremendous speed, was right on John's heels. John made it to the Devil's fifteen-yard line before Halen pulled him down. "Yeah, yeah, yeah!" Halen was psyched up as he lay there on top of John. Cade, angry now, slung Halen to the side and roared, "That was a lucky one, wait until the next carry, boy!"

"Screw you, whitey!" Halen screamed as he pumped his fist in the air, taunting John. Cade then pushed him hard with both hands; Halen sprawled backward and finally slid on his bottom at least ten yards on the wet and slippery field. Both teams ran on the field to join the skirmish; chaos broke out. It took ten minutes for the referees to restore order. The Nighthawks were given a fifteen-yard penalty for unsportsmanlike conduct. John, not caring about the penalty and the ball being placed at the Daredevils' thirty-yard line, just wanted his hands on the ball.

"Come on, Coach, I can do it!" John screamed as he stood on the sidelines, anxious to get back in the contest. "Wait, son, I have an idea, the Daredevils look tired," Gus said, his mouth twitching with anticipation. Gus patted John on the rear in an effort to calm his running back. Coach Thompson now called on seldom-used fullback Guy LaStone. LaStone, who stood at five foot seven and weighed 170 pounds, was a handful. Not much speed, but he had excellent power up the middle. His handsome features were always overshadowed by his powerful and muscular physique. As Gus put in LaStone, who wore his blonde hair in a ponytail, the play sent in with the fullback was two straight rushes.

Orosco yelled the cadence to the center, Ventura; and after the ball was snapped into Orosco's hand, he deftly faked going into the pocket. Then, as sweet as sugar, he stuffed the ball into the arms of LaStone. As LaStone took the handoff and headed up the middle, you could almost feel the shoulder pads connecting as the Daredevils stuck it to number 26. LaStone drug them to the thirty-five. Again, the ball was given to LaStone, and he earned another four yards. Getting the first down completed, Gus sent in Peal. It was possibly Peal's last play as a Nighthawk. "Do your thing, Peal!" Gus yelled, his palms sweating as he relayed the play to Peal. "Pass play, Peal." Gus wanted Peal to do something special. Cade, ever anxious, waited for the coach to call his number. Orosco, after Peal got in the huddle, asked, "What's the play, Peal?"

Peal quickly answered, "In the air, up the middle to me." Peal was nervous yet ready. "Four forty-seven, hut, hut, hut, hike!" Orosco screamed the cadence. Peal as soon as the ball was snapped—as he was on the right side of the field—sprinted ten yards and cut to the middle of the field. In full stride now, Peal looked in Orosco's direction. He saw the ball already coming, a perfect spiral. Peal skied as the ball was thrown slightly higher than arm's reach. He caught it and tucked it into his chest. At that moment, Halen stuck Peal and stuck him hard. You could hear the crowd let out a loud, "Oooh." Peal hit the natural grass hard and awkwardly, but he hung on to the ball. The officials spotted the ball at the ten. Larry was ecstatic as a fellow brother of the oppressed jogged off the field, seemingly unfazed by the tremendous hit of Halen. Gus hugged Peal and screamed, "Dammit, son, you keep making catches like that, and one day, it may pay off for you!"

"Thanks, Coach." Peal was all smiles. Coach then screamed, "Get in there, Cade, go to the right side!" The ball was given to Cade. He promptly lost four yards, but he held on to the ball. The crowd was standing now; it couldn't wait for the last quarter. Two more tries and Cade barely made it to the original line of scrimmage. This brought about a slight chorus of boos, but Coach left Cade in anyway.

Orosco, taking charge once in the huddle, called the last play. "Okay, guys, fourth and goal. We've got to do it, quarterback sweep!" The team lined up, Cade went to his usual position at tailback, and LaStone got to his place at fullback. When the play was called, Orosco faked a handoff to Cade. As he did that, LaStone charged up the middle. Orosco fell in stride behind him, an awesome display of power was shown. LaStone took out at least three defensive linemen opening the hole for Harman—touchdown Nighthawks. The score read, "Daredevils

13, Nighthawks 6." After a failed extra-point try, the Nighthawks kicked off. Daredevils took it at the Nighthawks' twenty-five. At the third quarter, both teams took a needed breather. Coach Thompson was proud of his Nighthawks but wanted something extra, and he let his men know it. "Look, kids, we have a chance for greatness at the middle school level, don't let it slip away!" Gus was almost foaming at the mouth. A win today and he could be called up for the college ranks.

The fourth quarter got under way. Gus called Larry back after the team had trotted out onto the field. "Now look, son, we may not see things eye to eye; but listen, if we win today, we'll get to wear gold-plated rings with our names on them, as well as a big trophy for the school display case. Now, don't you want that honor?" Pleased, Larry yelled, "Shit yeah, Coach!" Realizing his point being taken, Thompson ordered Larry, "Now, get in there and stick!" Thompson felt he could put all his marbles on Williams. Joseph Alexander, the Daredevils' quarterback who, at fourteen, stood a shade under six feet, was arguably the best runner among all middle school quarterbacks. He called cadence to his center, "Seven fourteen, seven fourteen, three thirty-one, hut, hut, hut, hike!" The Daredevils, known for their running game, weren't to be taken lightly. Even though Wilburton had the most talented core of linebackers among the competition, Gus was worried.

As Alexander, the shy but quick-thinking passer, took the ball from center, he quickly faked a handoff and went up the middle. A quick juke to the left froze Wilburton's front line so badly that they collided with each other. He then faked Myers and Luwinski and headed downfield. Greydog, on the opposite side of the play, now had to catch up. If it weren't for Hillman, who doubled as a defensive back, Alexander would have walked the field. As Hillman read the play, he charged right for the 130-

pound junior express. "Clack, clack." Hillman stood Alexander up. The two resembled two rams locked in battle. Williams, catching up to the two, was headed right for the backside of Alexander. The officials blew the play dead to prevent injury, Daredevil ball at the fifty. Fifteen-yard gain.

Daredevils' coach Roger Altobond knew Thompson well. The two played at Nebraska together, seemingly, centuries ago. Thompson's tactics as coach were the same as they were back in his playing days—pound, pound, pound. Coach Altobond was grateful to the officials for not letting things get out of hand. The Daredevils failed to score. Wilburton, receiving the ball after a weak kick, took it at their own thirty-five yard line. Trailing by only a touchdown, the Nighthawks knew that if they could score and make the extra point, they would lead. Gus called time-out. During the break, Coach informed the Nighthawks of their good fortune. "Let's run the clock as much as possible, men. Now, on this series, I want two quick ten-to twenty-yard pass attempts." He then turned to Cade. "Look, Cade, please, no fumbles."

Cade, up for the challenge, screamed in the cold, "Gotcha, Coach!"

Both teams lined up. A crucial series now, the Nighthawks were in a do-or-die situation. Orosco called for the ball, "Three thirty-seven, three thirty-seven, hut, hut, hike!" Cade, not much of a receiver in this stage of his football career, wanted to get out of the backfield on this play. After Orosco called the play and took the center, he calmly floated in the pocket. The Nighthawk front line did a perfect job of protecting Orosco. Ventura kept two pesky Daredevil defenders at bay. Orosco spotted Cade alone at the fifty-yard line; he threw John a bullet. The ball seemed to take forever, but there was no question when he caught it that only a few seconds had elapsed. "Oomph," Cade let out air as the ball hit him on the numbers. He then cradled the ball. The crowd stood. Off and running now, Cade was ahead of his blockers by some fifteen yards, yet Cade had to sprint toward the goal line anyway. Going top speed now, Cade growled trying to get all he could out of the play. Out of the corner of his eyes, as he looked back, Cade noticed Halen. He turned on the juice even more. Peal, trying to cover Cade, went for Halen. As he caught up to the lightning-quick runners, he legally took out Halen. This left Cade all alone, twenty, ten, touchdown, Nighthawks! Every Nighthawk slapped Peal's helmet as he trotted back to the sidelines. A smiling Peal didn't mind the ringing sensation in his ears. Gus yelled, "Peal, remind me to buy you lunch one day, son!"

"Anytime, Coach." Peal really felt part of things, even with his dislike for Cade, he did it for the benefit of the team. Greydog, as Peal came near, silently said, "All praise, Peal."

"All praise, Greydog." The two gave each other high fives. With a little over four minutes left in the eight-minute quarters, Thompson ordered Myers to kick it deep and high. "No returns, gentlemen!" As Alvin trotted to his position, he yelled to Ventura, "Chest high, Ventura." Ventura, concentrating on blocking, only nodded his head. As the ball was snapped, it went low. Angry now, Myers still had the ability to grab and kick it before the defenders got close enough to block it. A high kick off the side of Myers's kicking foot. "Dammit!" Myers screamed as the ball slowly descended to Halen at the Daredevils' forty. But before the speed demon broke loose, Luwinski, who played two roles, was already downfield. He hammered Halen. The slender Halen never knew what hit him; he coughed up the ball. It took a Nighthawk bounce back to their own twenty-five yard line before going out of bounds. Halen, still on the ground, had to have assistance on the field. It was a good hit; no penalty was called. This angered Altobond, who yelled at the officials for an illegal hit. Finally, when things settled, the ball was spotted at the twenty-three-yard line of the Devils. Coach Thompson reinforced his opinion verbally. Jokingly, he stated, "Anybody who lets this game get away, I'll beat him." Everyone laughed but Peal, Hillman, and Williams; they took it to heart. Gus, realizing his error, apologized to the trio. On a brighter note, he added, "Now, let's get out there and win!" The Nighthawks, feeling the title, were ready to hold the powerful Daredevils, who had upset the Cotton Razorblades two weeks prior for the right to this game.

    Alexander silently feared the Nighthawk defense. With only eighth-grade players, Wilburton's juniors would have to wait until next year. "Four fourteen, four fourteen, hut, hut, hut hike!" Alexander deftly went into the pocket; he then brilliantly handed off to menacing fullback, David Wilson. Though he was not too bright and out of shape because of his being expelled for fighting, Wilson, at an even two hundred pounds, still commanded attention. He went right up the middle; he knocked the burly Erik Turner over seemingly without effort. Still trudging up the middle, Wilson saw the linebackers of Wilburton coming right at him. Greydog hit first, he bounced off Wilson, yet Wilson felt all of the hit. Wilson, now almost out of breath, kept moving forward. Luwinski gave him a shoulder pad to the ribs, nothing doing. Wilson still moved ahead, and now it was Myers turn. Myers wrapped both arms around Wilson's ankles as Myers dove to the ground. Greydog slammed into Wilson again; Wilson, with Myers holding his ankles, had no choice but to go down, eight-yard gain. Luwinski had gone for the strip, but Wilson hung on to the ball. Wilson, though a powerful runner, was now gasping for air. If it weren't for his attitude, the Daredevils may have ran away with the contest. Yet the boyish-looking fifteen-year-old, with the missing two front teeth and deep voice, really hurt his team. Altobond had to spell his bruiser, who hadn't been a factor at all in this contest. Wilson, who knew of Greydog from the South Side, led the middle school league in rushing the first eight games until his mishap with a school security guard.

Under three minutes left, Altobond had no choice but to go in the air. Young quarterback Alexander's reliability was questionable, especially under this sort of pressure. Coach Altobond felt it slipping away. *Damn Thompson seems to get all the breaks.* Young Alexander seemed to handle the pressure beautifully until he put it up in the air. A measly toss, no farther than ten yards, was well out of the reach of a receiver. The ball squiggled out of bounds. Third and seven. Desperate, Altobond called for a quarterback sweep. Alexander, up for the challenge, tried to use his speed; but with Wilburton's core of linebackers speed, they chased him out of bounds for a five-yard gain. The teams were informed: two minutes left in regulation. A yard and the Daredevils would have first down. Coach Thompson called time-out. Emphasizing defense, the coach wanted every defender lined up front. Knowing they would call on number 24, Wilson, Thompson stressed this to his linebackers. It was possibly their last play of the season, and the Daredevils were ready. Alexander called for the ball, and instead of the anticipated handoff to Wilson, Alexander tried to go over the top for two yards. Turner and Luwinski weren't fooled; they met Alexander in the air and drove him back for a two-yard loss. It was now Nighthawks' football. Not having any time-outs left, the Daredevils were forced to watch Wilburton run out the clock. Although the Daredevils were cochamps with Northside last year, this time, however, Wilburton had to share with no one.

Tears steamed down the Daredevils faces as they shook hands with the new champs. Wilson spotted Larry during both teams' sportsmanship handshakes. The two men shook hands. Larry then asked Wilson to meet him at Seal's one day to talk. The crowd, mostly Daredevil fans, still cheered wildly for Wilburton, this year's darling of middle school competition. Before leaving the field with the players, Coach Thompson was barely able to compose himself, but he still had the presence of mind to instruct his players.

"I know you're cold with this weather, but who cares right! Before we hit the team bus, let's savor the moment. We're the champs, men!" Everyone then began singing the Nighthawks' team song together.

That evening at the Cade home during dinner, John was all smiles. Barbara, still angry at her son for not studying regularly, scolded John as he chomped on his food. "John, what are you going to major in high school?" As he finished eating the last piece of roast beef on his plate, John contemplated on the question, then he finally spoke up, "Aerodynamics, Mom." Barbara was impressed, yet still she had to ask, "What will you do, build or fly planes, John?" John, always surprised at his mom's ability to read his mind, said as such, "You have been reading my mind again, Mom." John jokingly added, "I'm going to have to move soon, or I'll have no peace in my life." Harold finally got in the conversation. "Eat, son, being the champ probably leaves you with some appetite." Harold then began eating again.

As the family lay reclining after their evening meal, they began going over the plans for John's future. With some seven months left at Wilburton, and football being over for the year, John still had to stay focused on education. Harold, slightly worried about John's schoolwork, reinforced Barbara's concern. "Son, don't forget about your homework assignments. It's the key to success. You know I'd be nowhere without doing mine."

Thinking on the matter, Harold suggested, "Maybe you see Carolyn so often—" John couldn't believe his ears. "Dad, no!" Carolyn was the reason for John's dream. John began to sulk. Barbara intervened. "Son, we love you, and we want the best for you and Carolyn."

"Oh, all right, I'll do my dumb homework regularly from now on, I promise." John was worried now. "Okay, son, you gave us your word." Harold reminded his son. He also knew John wouldn't lie on purpose.

CHAPTER 7
GOOD-BYE ARTHUR

Arthur had been waiting for this information for at least a year, and now he had it. A gang of white youth from the Westside had been the shooters that killed young Sharkey and Juanita. Now, all Arthur had to do was get in touch with Greydog. "When I get hold of my boy, Larry, I will find out what kind of soldiers I have," the excited Arthur said to himself. The gang had reached over ten thousand during the past year. Arthur could sense they were green, but they were very eager to prove themselves to each other.

The meetings had to be held every night, for two hours each session. With the heavy bolted doors, it gave them ample time to hide the weapons when need be. When the police would visit, they were at first concerned at so many youth congregating together; but with the weapons out of sight and secured, no one grew suspicious. Things went rather smoothly. Arthur informed law officials that his establishment was called Help the Troubled Youth. This went so well with lawmen that they even suggested to spend time with the boys, but at Arthur's insistence that this would make the boys bashful, the city gave Arthur its blessing.

At Terran's prodding, Arthur had recruited some of his ex-felon friends to supervise the teenagers. Arthur still considered young Greydog to be the leader. "With that boy's ambition, he could be president." Arthur was very proud of young JoJo.

Thinking to himself about Larry before calling him, Arthur felt that the boy could handle the situation. As he dialed the number, the phone rang several times before Wilma answered the phone. "Hello." It startled X. "Uh, hi, Ms. Williams, is little Jo there?" Arthur felt the tension in the air.

Angry at the name she heard, Wilma let Arthur know it. "You know, I don't like people calling him that. What do you want anyway?" Wilma felt trouble now, but she didn't want to anger Larry, not when he was doing so well in school. Thinking fast, Arthur calmed Wilma, "I just want to congratulate him on winning the game today, ma'am." It worked, Wilma relaxed a little and said, "Okay, but don't keep him too long, he's eating supper." Pleased, Arthur responded, "Yes, ma'am." As Wilma fetched Larry, he quickly picked up the receiver. "Who this?"

"Easy, Greydog, it's Arthur. Listen, meet me at the warehouse tomorrow. I have something for you." Edgy at the suggestion and not wanting to get Wilma scared, Larry played it cool. "Okay, I'll be there, X, but right now, I have to go, I have some homework to do." Pleased at Larry's obvious smarts, Arthur bid farewell. Then remembering his words to Wilma, he said, "By the way, congratulations on the big game. It will probably be in all the local newspapers. I saw that flying white boy on your team tearing up ground." Larry couldn't help but smile, then added, "Yes, the boy definitely has some of us in him." The two hang up their respective phones, laughing. As Larry sat down to eat, Wilma felt good about her son. "It's cold out tonight, are you going out, boy?" Wilma, face frowning in worry, looked at Larry, who replied, "No, Ma, I have homework that won't wait."

"Good, son, I want you to help me one day, you remember that." As she observed Larry eating, Wilma knew he was her only hope out of South Side and the mean streets, but she had to wait. Sometimes, she even felt it wouldn't be bad if Larry sold dope. "Seem like they don't have room enough in their pockets with all that money," Wilma chuckled to herself. Then, more serious, she knew she couldn't lose Larry now. Tired of thinking, Wilma excused herself and went to her room. "Good night, Ma."

Feeling the love Larry had for her, Wilma smiled then softly said, "Good night, son." After he finished eating, Larry cleared the table.

Their budget, ground beef always seemed to pop up, but as famished as Larry was after school each day, it didn't matter, hot food was hot food. Larry then went to his room and brought out his schoolbooks. A bright boy, Larry already studied prealgebra and advanced English. His craving for a law degree kept him from straying away from his studies. After going over his lessons, Larry studied his copies of the United States Constitution. He received copies from the public library.

Larry never failed to remember the nicer sections of South Side when he did his studies and how nice a lot of blacks who lived in that section were. Reality always seemed to smack him in the face. The apartment he and Wilma shared was still ghetto. Thinking to himself, Larry murmured, "Boy, you just can't win. Now Grandma wants me to help her. I have to do something." As he looked at the clock above the dirty white seventies refrigerator, Larry noticed the time. "Ten thirty, damn, I better get some sleep. It's going to be a long trip to see X tomorrow." Larry wondered what Arthur had to tell him as he retired to his room.

"I have been waiting on you, Greydog, you're late," Arthur teased his comrade. Arthur was all smiles as he greeted Larry. The two men entered the warehouse. Arthur, who had patiently waited outside the building for Larry, now shoved a *Chicago Sun Times* in front of Larry. Wilburton had made the front page of the sports section, which read: "Wilburton Captures Middle School Football Title." It went on to read, "Mayor Lauded with Success of New Schools." Both men looked at each other and yelled, "All praise to revolt!" Now that they were inside of the building, Arthur broke the news to Larry, who was ecstatic. Larry yelled, "Is that right, man! Let's go get them punks!" Larry broke skin; he had bit his lip so hard. The taste of blood filled Larry's mouth as he looked at Arthur X with eager expectations. Arthur, sensing his friend's anxiety, had to slow Larry's mind down. "Hold yourself, Greydog, tonight. I know the white boy's routine; they are the European swine of that area. I found out your boy Sharkey had beaten some white boy out of some drugs and money, and the white boys scorched him for it." Stunned at the news, Larry was speechless. "Sharkey . . . ," Larry said out loud in disbelief. Feeling the tension in the air, Arthur tried to reassure his young friend. He suggested to Larry, "We'll go over to my apartment and spend the rest of the day there, is that all right, young JoJo?" Larry, never having the honor to visit Arthur's place, quickly responded, "Hell yes, man, I want to see what rich people live like anyway." Arthur chuckled then added, "Let's lock up, and as soon as Lisa comes to pick us up, we'll be fine." The two braved the cold, icy November weather. Last year's winter, as brutal as it was, seemed like decades ago instead of months.

Lisa pulled to the curb. Arthur opened the door of the two-door affair and ushered young Larry in the backseat. He had already informed Greydog to keep silent so Lisa wouldn't become alarmed and go to the authorities. Once inside the Northside apartment complex, which housed Arthur's high-rise apartment, Larry was impressed from the meticulous way it was kept to the specially designed dark brown wooden floor. The view of the lake captivated Greydog. He felt that one day he could afford this kind of luxury if he could just keep going in football. Arthur gave Larry a tour of the three-bedroom job; Larry playfully asked to move in. Arthur took it to heart and spoke of it happening one day. Larry was flattered, but he assured Arthur he was okay being with Grandma. They went to Arthur's study; once inside, Arthur locked the door and turned on the air humidifier. Opening a drawer on a dynamic-looking chestnut furniture set, Arthur pulled out an ounce of marijuana. "The good stuff," Arthur said as he gave Larry a whiff. "We'll blow some and then get some rest." Thinking of Wilma, Arthur asked, "Is your grandma going to be all right?" With his mouth watering at the scent of the strong-smelling herb, Arthur's question snapped Larry back to reality. "Yes, she will be all right," Larry blurted out. Arthur began rolling the marijuana into intoxicating cigarettes. After he finished, Arthur lit one. Being an experienced smoker, Arthur inhaled then hung on to the smoke, then exhaled. Afterward, he passed the joint to Larry. Nervous, Larry came clean. "I never smoked this shit before, X, but I do drink a little beer." Arthur quickly went to the small closet in the room and grabbed a fifth of the Hennessy he had stashed there. "We in like Flinn, young JoJo."

Larry motioned, "All praise to revolt." Arthur gave Larry a high five and then scolded him for letting the joint go out. "Hit it hard, man, I want to get good and high before the hit we are going to do on them white boys tonight!" Taking Arthur's advice, Larry lit the sweet-smelling cannabis and hit it hard. As the smoke expanded, it felt like someone was using an air hose inside his chest. Larry coughed hard and long. Arthur exploded in small chuckles. Remembering his first time getting high, Arthur told his friend, "You will be all right, just get ready for the buzz now." Larry silently felt the point was well taken.

At seven thirty that night, Arthur called his boy Kank whom he met on the streets during his hustling days. Arthur waited patiently while the phone rang. After at least eight rings, Arthur grew impatient. "Damn, where is the bastard!" Finally, he got an answer, a high-pitched but hard-sounding male voice answered the receiver. "Who the hell is it and it better be good!" Arthur relaxed, knowing he found Kank. "What's up, old man, I thought you was lying on top of some woman or something." Not to be denied, Kank, in his cool street voice came back at Arthur, "Shit, I was, nigger. I found this broad at a party last night. Bitch is sleep now though. I thought you woke her ass up with all the phone ringing." Kank jokingly pulled Arthur's pud. Arthur, serious now, shot back at Kank, "Bring that car you told me about over to the warehouse on 103rd. You, me, and my main man, young JoJo, have some business to do." The ever-ready Kank, never one to turn down a challenge, promised Arthur that he'd be there. "All right, X, give me two hours." Arthur felt the lights go on in his head. "Perfect, Kank, we'll be there." As Arthur hung up the phone, he looked at the time, not quite eight o'clock in the evening yet. Arthur looked over at Larry, who now lay sprawled on the ice-blue carpet snoring. Arthur could see slight spittle coming out of the corner of Larry's mouth. "Damn, boy's stoned out of his ass! I'll let him sleep for another hour, then he's going to have to get ready for action."

Kank, also known as Thomas Jones, waited patiently in the rear of the warehouse, which was concealed from traffic and right out of city boundary. Kank stood a shade over six feet, was slender, and with a light complexion. Kank was not a very attractive man; his gapped teeth and pockmarked face always made him the last man on a girl's list, yet his ability as a crack dealer kept him with armloads of females. Their crack addiction also helped in their decision to spend time with the ex-felon. Kank, while living in New York, served four years on Rikers Island for drug distribution. After waiting for seemingly hours, Arthur and Greydog showed up. Kank looked at his cheap timepiece. "Quarter to ten, it's about time." As Arthur opened the door of the Mustang, he and Larry exited the vehicle. Larry stepped away from the vehicle; Arthur held the door open so he could give Lisa a good-bye kiss and tell her not to worry, he'd be home soon. A concerned Lisa bid her farewell and sped off into traffic. As Lisa drove off, Terran showed up. Kank's distrust for all non-black Americans was eased by Arthur, who had earlier pleaded with Kank that Terran was on their side and to be easy. And from what Arthur explained about Terran gave Kank the feeling that Mr. Habib was a terrorist all the way. As Kank would say, "Silky smooth." The four men silently and easily entered the rear entrance of the large building. Larry, still feeling the effects of the alcohol and weed, couldn't help but be scared. Terran spoke briefly with Arthur before going into his office. Arthur then unlocked the large industrial storage boxes. He came out of it with three AK-47 rifles. He handed Kank and Larry one each, and he kept the other one for himself. Seemingly seconds later, Terran came out with a box containing live ammunition. He instructed each person to load their weapons. Larry thought he would faint; he was so excited. Arthur spoke to Larry, "Tell no one of this, little Jo, not even fellow members of the oppressed, got that?" Larry began to feel anger boil in him because of Arthur not saying anything to Kank, slightly nodded his head once.

The loading of rounds in the banana clip magazines echoed loudly in the empty warehouse. When each man had loaded two magazines at thirty rounds for each clip, Arthur stood up to yell, "All praise to revolt!" The duet of Kank and Larry sang back, "All praise to revolt!" Arthur then signaled to Kank to check outside and see if the coast was clear. After looking outside carefully both ways, Kank gave the thumbs up. The three men quickly moved. With no one watching, they got the weapons into the slightly banged-up '91 green stolen Ford van. Inconspicuous as the vehicle was, the blackness of the men would make them stick out; but being that a lot of blacks lived in the Westside area, arousing suspicion wasn't a big concern. The fact that Sharkey and Juanita were killed at an Oak Park residence helped Arthur to find out who the shooters were.

According to Arthur's informant, they belonged to the supremacist Aryan group who partied on the Westside on the weekends. Terran, already outside in his car, waited for the trio. Terran, who wanted to observe the men in action, waited patiently for the van to leave the warehouse then he would follow it. Arthur looked at his watch as the van pulled into traffic. "Eleven forty-two, almost midnight. Perfect. Kank, take your time, let them get good and drunk."

"Sure thing," Kank hollered back at X. "Just hope no cops pull our ass over." Arthur, looking around at traffic, chuckled and added, "You sure got that right." He commented with conviction, "That's all we need, more time in the penitentiary." He and Kank both had to ease the tension by laughing. They both knew the hell of prison would be their home if they were caught with the assault rifles. Larry, trembling now, didn't see a damn thing funny.

A little after midnight, they made it to Austin, a nice suburban area on the West Side. Still searching, they drove through the industrial districts. Finally, they slowed as the van entered the old and decaying residential areas. Arthur asked Kank to stop next to some abandoned apartments. Kank quickly turned off the headlights of the vehicle. "All right, boys, this is it!" Arthur said, clearing his throat in the process. Even with the cold, the men were sweating. They got out of the vehicle and, almost turtlelike, walked upon a vacant apartment complex. Weapons ready, the trio continued to inch forward, then suddenly, out of nowhere, someone yelled, "Watch out, here they come!" Frantic, Arthur realized it was a setup. He yelled, "Open fire!" Kank and Larry began firing wildly in to the dark. Arthur, firing at the direction of muzzle flashes, screamed, "Hit the dirt and fire!" But before he could get down, Arthur took four slugs in the chest.

 Larry, now on his second clip, vomited at the sight of Arthur X jerking as the bullets ripped through him. Kank, unfazed, kept his finger on the trigger of the fully automatic weapon; he threw in his second clip. Picking his shots, Kank noticed the enemy's fire wasn't as great now, but he wasn't going to give up yet. Larry, his nerves calm now, could somehow see when bodies were falling in the barely visible building. Kank, getting Larry's attention, motioned with a finger across the neck for Larry to stop firing. Greydog obliged. The firing had ceased. The two were eating concrete for all of five minutes slowly rose up. Cautious, they moved slowly toward Arthur, who lay motionless on the ground. When they saw Arthur, Larry was crushed. Arthur, or what was left of him, lay there in a twisted heap. Blood oozed from the wounds. Kank, in a humane gesture, closed Arthur's eyes with his fingers. Before he was able to get to the building to finish off any survivors, Kank noticed headlights coming. "Get down!" he screamed at Larry. As they got down and the vehicle came closer, Kank realized it was Terran. The quick-thinking Kank grabbed Arthur's weapon and spare banana clip.

Since Arthur had no identification, Kank didn't bother going through Arthur's pockets. Terran motioned for the men to come on, then he quickly popped the trunk from the inside of the car. Both men threw the empty weapons in the trunk, separate from the clips. Larry then jumped in to the backseat of the luxury import. Kank, the experienced one, went to the van and, almost ghostlike, wiped the door handles. He went inside the vehicle, smearing everything he could. Seconds later, he jumped in to the front passenger's seat of the beige '88 Mercedes. Terran quickly headed for the expressway. Seconds later, the area was swarming with law enforcement. No one spoke during the ride back to the warehouse. When they arrived on 103rd, Kank spoke first. "Let me use your cell phone, Terran. I have to make a phone call."

"Sure," Terran said unemotionally, then he turned his attention to Larry. "Come inside, my friend, we have to talk." Still in shock, Larry could only nod his head and say, "Okay, man." Once inside Terran's office, Terran sized up the young man who was now a killer. "You did well, what do they call you?" In disbelief at Terran's obvious ignorance, Larry could only say, "Greydog, man."

"Of course, how could I have forgotten." Terran went on, "Now that Arthur's dead, how do you feel?" Terran observed Larry, hoping to catch a weakness. Knowing he couldn't show his true emotions, Larry feigned toughness. "I'm ready, Tee." Pleased at the young man's integrity, Terran nodded his approval. Kank interrupted by banging on the door. "Hey, in there, I put the weapons inside by the storage box, and my ride will be here any second, so I'm out of here!" Opening the door, Terran shook Kank's hand. "Get in touch with me tomorrow, Mr Kank?"

"Yes, Kank's my name. Later, till Monday." Kank then vanished into the darkness. Back to Larry, Terran, concerned, asked, "It's well past one in the morning, aren't your parents concerned?" Larry, surprised at Terran's sensitivity, responded, "It's just Ma and me, as long as I come home alive, she won't fuss."

"Good," Terran then seized the moment. "Obviously, you can see we need a new leader. Before Mr. X's untimely death, he spoke well of you." Not being able to pronounce his *Rs* easily, Terran did as best as his skills allowed. Larry got the message anyway. "So what do you want from me, Mr. Terran?" Terran thoughtfully held his hands together, then he added, "I want you to be the leader now. With your desire to revolt against this country, you are an obvious selection." Larry, swelling with pride despite his pain for Arthur X, accepted his new position. Pleased, Terran went on, "Now, you will need money. I will give you a false employment record, and I'll pay you out of my pocket. Fifteen hundred dollars a month." Terran knew that too much money too soon would get someone suspicious of one so young and poor instantly becoming rich. Feeling like a hundred-pound weight had been lifted from his shoulders, Larry let go of a broad grin. Careful not to put too much pressure on this naive teenager, Terran further instructed his troop, "Larry, let Mr. Kank pick his men to be in charge of the other youth. We have grown to at least ten thousand troops. Can you share leadership, Mr. Dog?" Beaming now, Larry complied, "Yes, Mr. Terran, I can do it!"

"Excellent. Now, I better get you home. Could you wait outside my office? I'll be with you shortly."

"Okay, Mr. Terran." Larry shut the door of the tiny barely furnished office. He stepped out into the cold, darkened warehouse. Terran made a call. He left a message on the other party's answering machine. "Come and pick up the supplies in every warehouse by 6:00 a.m.," Then he used the secret code words "the boy has lost his dog." Which meant possible search of the buildings Terran operated. Terran felt confident his men from his native Middle Eastern home wouldn't let him down. He then turned his attention to getting Larry home. By the time he was inside the apartment, it was well after two in the morning. After locking the door, Larry quietly went to his room, being careful so as to not disturb Grandma. He briefly went over his homework. As he did, Larry's emotions started to flow, and the tears began streaming down. First, Sharkey and Juanita, now Arthur. Larry's refusal to attend Sharkey's or Juanita's funeral surprised no one. Silently, through tears as he lay stretched out on his bed, Larry felt there was no way he would accept Arthur as dead. Arthur, in Larry's mind, would always be a part of revolt. Exhausted, Larry turned off his light and forced himself to sleep.

    Monday morning, with football season over, John relaxed a little. As he slowly climbed out of bed at 5:00 a.m., he began his regime of calisthenics. The push-ups and sit-ups helped John to stay mentally sharp. After thirty minutes of this, John went over his schoolwork. Being a little behind in his general math, John knew he would have to play catch-up the rest of the year. Now in his second year at Wilburton, John could feel himself growing. He now stood five foot ten. "Man, I'm taller than Mom by at least two inches." His frame constantly putting on more weight didn't surprise John. "With my appetite, I hope my weight doesn't balloon to over two hundred." A knock on the door snapped John out of his world. "Breakfast is ready, John, come and get it while it's hot." "Be right there, Mom." John then took a look at his toy model air force jets. Thinking, he surmised, *One day, they might come to life.* After breakfast, Harold suggested to his son, "Like a ride to school, John?" In between bites, John gladly accepted.

"Sure, Dad, but what about Carolyn?" John patiently asked. "Can we pick her up too?"

"Why not, son? After breakfast give her a call so she'll be ready for us."

"Sure, and thanks a million, Dad." John then dove into his meal.

The incident was printed by several Chicago papers. Larry, up early this morning despite only a couple of hours' sleep, stayed glued to the television set. Finally, the news anchorwoman reported the incident. "Police, after a call around midnight reporting shots being fired, arrived on the scene and discovered six men dead in an abandoned building in the West Side area. Five bodies were found in one of the vacant apartments, and one lay dead outside the complex. There was no motive found for the slayings except that one was black. The other five were known to frequent the area regularly, according to witnesses." The anchor went on to report, "There were weapons lying near the bodies on the inside of the dilapidated apartment, and police surmised that an assault weapon, possibly AK-47, was used in the attack. They don't have suspects at this time." Larry turned the television set off as the anchor was ready to say, "Anyone with information, contact the police." Larry let it soak in. "I've killed people!" Larry felt different, almost like a superpower flowing through him. Minutes later, the ringing telephone brought Larry back to reality. He answered it without fear. "Hello." It was Edbert. "Are you going to school today, Greydog?" Larry knew Edbert wasn't serious, but he replied anyway. "Yes, man, shit, I'm not living poor all of my life. I want to learn as much as I can." Larry, the ever-mature one about his education let Edbert know it. Edbert was grinning on the other end because he knew he had information Larry didn't. "Listen, Greydog, high school representatives are coming to all middle schools, and they're giving us a choice on which high school to go to." This excited Larry, who responded to Edbert, "I know the school I want, but I have to speak to Quenlin about this. We're both going to the same school."

Edbert answered Larry, "Peal and myself have been doing some talking too." Then Edbert changed the subject. "You playing ball in high school, Greydog, because I'm not. I'm getting educated, and then my mother and me are going to leave Chicago." Surprised at Edbert's sudden change of heart, Larry sadly asked, "What about revolt?"

"That's why we are leaving, mother heard Cornell and me plotting, and she is not having it." Edbert felt sheepish about the situation, but he had to tell Larry.

"Damn, Ed, I wish you luck. What about Peal?" Larry asked, concerned.

"You will have to ask him about it," Edbert suggested. Then as quick as he called, Edbert ended the conversation. "Have to go, Larry, I'll talk to you at school." They both hung up their respective phones.

That day in school, the late-November weather was a reminder of the shattering December cold. A high wind today didn't hamper the kids' spirits. Everyone who attended Wilburton would be there. The students were ecstatic over being called the champions. Even the cold weather couldn't suppress their joy. Gus, who specifically coached football, was able to take a much-needed vacation. Kids would have to wait to be counseled by him as he was the designated counselor in the off-season. The school had all the eighth-grade students meet in the school auditorium, which was a lavish affair. Cushion seats with Nighthawk blue, also a large screen for video purposes. It resembled a nice theater. Mr. Dan Peebles, the school principal, addressed the students. Peebles, a thin graying man with a balding head who wore thick glasses, didn't know why he chose being a principal over a teacher. Being a principal was boring, yet he always wore tailor-made suits, which seemed to separate him from the other faculty. Today he decided to wear his light brown three-piece suit. It definitely stood out next to Peebles' pale skin. He addressed the students, "People, may I have your attention." Then, in his larger-than-life voice, he spoke of the Nighthawks. "I want to welcome the city champions of the Cactus League, our own Nighthawks. Give them a hand." After the loud five-minute applause, the team was asked to stand on stage with Mr. Peebles.

The thirty-eight members were presented with their rings. There was nothing but teeth glowing from the stage. Then the large trophy, which stood almost three feet high, was represented to the school. After twenty minutes of yelling and screaming, Mr. Peebles, over the microphone, asked the students to cooperate and be quiet for a minute. "This is your big day, Nighthawks. We have representatives from the high school district who are here to assist you in your choice for high school next year." They explained to the students their choices for next year, which left Wilburton students very happy.

At home that night, John explained the situation to his parents. Harold, wanting to spare no expense on his son's education, asked John, "Is this what you really want, son? You know we could send you to a private school."

"No, Dad, I want to earn my life." John was adamant about not being a rich softy everyone picked on. Barbara, forever sensing the toughness of John, spoke out, "You know, Harold, he takes after you, don't spoil it for him." Curious, Barbara had to know. "What about Carolyn, son?" Thinking quickly, John said, "I'll speak to her soon, Mom, but right now I have studying to do." John excused himself from his parents and went to his bedroom.

The gang was in shock after they all found out about Arthur's death. Kank's men informed as many members as they could through the grapevine. Cornell cried when he heard the news; he couldn't believe the seemingly indestructible Arthur could let himself go out like that. Terran felt it all crumbling away; he canceled meetings for two weeks. He had to soothe Lisa, who threatened to go to the authorities until Terran assured her she would receive a settlement in the future. She had already used her pull as a lawyer to secure the money Arthur had in the bank. At first, she balked at Terran's proposal; but the look in Terran's eyes made Lisa realize, this was a do-or-die situation. Frightened for her life, she accepted his offer.

Larry, in his new position as leader, knew he had to concentrate on law and some military knowledge to be a real leader now that he was in charge.

CHAPTER 8
MOUNT WHITNEY

That summer before football tryouts at Whitney, John felt a little angry about the Dolphins' academic program. If it weren't for his dad's insistence to the school, John wouldn't have been eligible for space technology. Yet, as it stood, he was selected for higher education, but he had to wait until he became a sophomore before he could put on the football pads.

Carolyn, as always, wanted to be with her sweetheart Johnny. The two couldn't wait for school to start, knowing they were that much closer to going off to college after completing high school. Carolyn impatiently asked, "Let's go over our schedule again. We only have a couple of months before the big day." Wanting to enjoy summer vacation, John whined, "Come on, Carolyn, let's go swimming today." Carolyn, sensing a change in her friend, began to worry about him.

"You okay, John? You don't seem too concerned about your future." John, feeling it was time, finally spilled the marbles. "Listen, Carolyn, I can't participate in school sports this year, so maybe I'm a little upset, that's all." Carolyn, feeling better about things, let up. Then she stood up and went to her bedroom door and opened it. "Good, Mom and Dad are talking in the dining room." When she winked at the smiling John and motioned for him to come over, John hurriedly went to his girl. Carolyn put her arms around Cade. "Maybe this will help you feel better, tiger." Without hesitating, John kissed Carolyn deep and hard, his tongue exploring the newfound pleasure. Carolyn then began feeling awkward about the whole situation; she giggled and took a few steps back. "Now, hold on, John. What do you want to do, assault me?" John, horny as ever, went back to his chair and feigned innocence. "What did I do, ma'am?" Now feeling better about John's mental outlook, Carolyn gave in. "All right, let's go swimming, except you change in the restroom."

"Do I have to?" John laughingly asked. The two laughed so hard Sandy had to come in and check on them.

Larry began to relish his role as a leader even though he himself wasn't doing much leading. "Damn, I hope Terran knows what he's doing. All I do is talk to him about his ideas in the future." The gang had decreased to about six thousand after Arthur's death, and with a complete investigation by the authorities about the gang last winter, many youth stopped coming altogether. Kank had gotten many of his boys off the streets. Now men who loved violence were being recruited.

Terran, helpless now about the quality of youths joining, still kept his plan to cripple America in check. "There's no need to tell these imbeciles right now. I'd lose all control of the people." The six thousand men who still wanted to be a part of revolt were slowly persuaded by Kank to start doing illegal activities. Drug dealing hadn't started yet, but theft, robberies, and outright intimidation of innocent people of the city were beginning to be commonplace. Since they could no longer keep weapons stashed at the large warehouses, Terran suggested to each member to practice at home using broomsticks with small nails at the top to simulate sights of rifles. This sat well with most members because of the harsh penalties one received if caught using assault weapons. The men Kank wanted to help keep troops organized were from the same background as Kank. Kank, being second in command to Larry, didn't like taking orders from some wet-behind-the-ears teenager. Over thirty himself, Kank, in his estimation, wanted real men.

June 30, a restless Kank requested a meeting with Terran. The two agreed to meet at the warehouse on 103rd. The agreement was to meet there at 6:30 p.m. When Terran showed up, Kank was already there waiting. "My man, Terran," Kank slowly drawled, "how's things going?"

"It's okay, my friend, now let's go inside." The two shook hands and went into the building to Terran's small office. Seated in the only other chair in the small cubicle, Kank began to speak. "Look, my man, maybe you want this organization out of the goodness of your heart or maybe it's something you want out of this deal." Kank looked directly into Terran's eyes. Terran didn't flinch but insisted for Kank to go on. He did. "I have some damn tough people who could get things started. Man, we need a treasure, a strongman, and capable leaders." Kank cut himself short when Terran raised his finger. Terran, not worrying about being bugged, his men had already checked. Terran began speaking. "This is true, Mr. Kink?" Angrily, Kank corrected Terran. "Kank, man!" This made Terran smile, knowing he had gotten under the American's skin. Terran went on. "I've been handling all financial affairs, and we have yet to write a bad check." Kank interrupted. "I've got at least forty thousand people interested in joining, but we don't have room for them in the warehouses." This excited Terran, but he kept his cool as he questioned Kank, "What are your plans, Kank?"

"I have my boy, Luke, he's an accountant. Boy can turn shit into gold. Look, Terran," Kank went on, "I can't keep hiding the five-dollar-a-week dues money, and if we let the thousands of people join, that's a lot of loose money lying around." Terran, feeling good again, made a deal with Kank. "You let Mr. Williams be the leader. He is a positive image, and he's still young. I will let you lead the troops in practice, and you can bring your men into the gang, deal?" The two shook hands and then sang the song, "All praise to revolt!" Kank then said, "I'll call you when I get things situated, Terran." Kank then got up to leave, smiling to himself.

Larry had to sit out his freshmen year, team rules. Not surprisingly, he and Cade were the only Nighthawks to make the team. Peal decided he'd concentrate on basketball and track, but the rest were patted on the back with a thank-you-for-trying-out note. About the only good thing in it for Larry was that he was allowed to watch practices, which he did. As the weeks of the welcome summer months went by, Larry spent more of his time with Quenlin, who now shared the new apartment with Wilma and Larry. He did it with the money he received monthly from Terran. The family moved into a better location on far south in West Side, Chicago. Although rent was high, the apartment was a welcome relief from the crowded apartments on South Side. With his birthday passing that July, in which Larry turned fifteen, Quenlin, now fourteen, thought she'd give Larry a surprise birthday present. As the two lay in bed two weeks before school, Quenlin startled Larry. "Guess what, Greydog?"

Anxious, Larry whined, "What, girl?"

"I'm pregnant." Larry popped straight up on the bed. Feeling so good, he ran to tell Ma. He informed her about it. Wilma, ever wise, spoke to her son, "It's going to be a lot of responsibility, son. But I can use the company when you and Quenlin go off to school. Lord knows I don't like being alone."

Larry hugged Wilma and went back to Quenlin who now lay on the bed, silently crying. "What's wrong, babe? You should be happy." Larry, concerned about his girl, stroked Quenlin's hair. "I'm just thinking about Juanita and Sharkey." Then somberly, Quenlin asked, "Let's put some flowers on them and Arthur's grave, okay, Larry?" Feeling like a fool now for missing the funerals, Larry stayed silent. After some prodding by Quenlin, Larry finally agreed.

With the help of Terran, the bodies of Arthur, Sharkey, and Juanita were laid to rest across town at the Rosehill Cemetery. The two caught a taxi there the next day. With over five hundred dollars in his pockets, Larry politely asked the driver to wait once they arrived at the cemetery. After twenty minutes of searching, they found Sharkey's grave marker, then they found Juanita's headstone. Quenlin had purchased flowers from a local peddler, which she carefully put on each grave. As they searched for Arthur's headstone, Larry spotted Lisa. He yelled for her, and she turned around. She was startled at first, then she recognized who it was. She motioned for the two to come over. "Well hello, Larry, long time no see. How have you been?" Lisa studied the young man whom she felt knew more than he let on. "I've been fine. Quenlin and I are going to have a baby." Larry patted Quenlin's stomach. Lisa, getting down to business, stated, "There are some things of Arthur's that I have no use for. I'd like for you to have them if it's all right, Larry." After studying the expensive headstone of X and feeling the water coming, Larry could only meekly get out, "It would be okay."

Wondering about it, Lisa finally asked, "How did you two get here?" Quenlin spoke out, "By cab." After ten minutes of studying Arthur's grave, Lisa suggested that they take her car back to her apartment, and she'd give them a ride home. They both agreed. Larry then paid the cab driver the ninety-five-dollar fee, which made him groan, "Boy, I can't wait until I get my driver's license." He then caught up to the two girls, and the trio headed to Lisa's.

The two sleek-looking brief cases were locked, but Lisa gave Larry the keys. After Lisa hugged Larry and shot him a knowing stare, she asked Quenlin to take care of him, then she offered them a ride home. Larry opened the black one first then studied its contents. It blew Larry's young but experienced mind. "So this is why Arthur wanted to revolt." Larry, after going over each of the fifty pages of literature, was now convinced he was right for wanting to fight the system. One page about black queens stuck out in his mind, but a four-page story really startled him. It read how blacks were once world rulers and had governments and kings and how, sadly, they lost this prestigious position. It also told of a time in their history that over three million books had been burned. It went on to tell how blacks were blinded by slavery to the point of savagely killing each other. Larry was mesmerized by the cobweb-cleaning knowledge. After two hours of studying this material, called the five percent, Larry, a new man now, opened the other brief case, a sleek-looking brown hand carrier. Larry whistled. Inside there were at least five two-inch stacks of twenties. There was also a letter from Arthur, and it read, "My young JoJo, if you receive this information, it means I died and you lived. Well, if that's the case, I know you'll enjoy this. Don't worry about me, by now hell's invited me with open arms. Don't give up, Greydog! Do it for me, man, everybody will be counting on you. Use the knowledge to lead, not fool around. See you in hell. Love, X." Larry felt the butterflies coming, yet he couldn't put down the letter. Quenlin, ecstatic about seeing the money, already had one stack counted. "It's five thousand dollars in this stack!" She measured it against the other four stacks. "Larry, we have at least twenty-five thousand dollars here!"

"Good," Larry said. "Let's just keep a low profile and help Ma with some bills." Then he added, "With the money I get every month from Terran..." The two hugged. "We will be all right, Q." Larry acknowledged in his ever-deepening voice.

The first day at school at Mount Whitney, John was ready. Barbara, who wouldn't trade in the de Ville, insisted to John and Carolyn to let her drive them to school on the first day. John had informed Barbara that she couldn't park on Laflin Street because of school buses, the street would be too congested. Since she had two choices of either Jackson Boulevard or Adams Street, Barbara chose the less-crowded Adams. "Boy, Mom, I didn't think it would be this many students," John said nervously. "Don't worry, son, you study hard okay. I hear this school has great college prep courses, which will more than help you gain entrance into a university." Curious, Barbara had to ask, "What college are you going to anyway, son?"

"I really can't say, Mom. I have to go—come on, Carolyn—or we'll be late!" Barbara touched both kids and waited for them to shut the door, afterward they frantically waved good-bye to each other. John and Carolyn looked well in their matching blue jeans and brown pullover T-shirts, and the white boat sneakers gave them a preppy look. Taking a full schedule, John felt intimidated at some of his course subjects, especially precalculus and government politics. He and Carolyn said their good-byes. John was happy he and Carolyn had a chance to learn the school's classroom locations during the summer months. Now all they had to do was show up on time. The over eighteen hundred students did make things somewhat difficult to walk the hallways. As John entered his morning English class, he sighed, "Here we go again."

Larry caught a cab to school this morning. His white two-piece suit went splendid with the light blue suede leather mountain boots. The blue sun visor had Greydog looking like a young pimp. Quenlin decided she would do home studies for two years. An above-average intellectual girl, Quenlin trusted Larry completely. Excited about school, Larry majored in law at Whitney High. As hard as Larry studied, he still barely was excepted in the grueling course. It would be a long four years, Larry thought to himself as he opened his text book in his morning psychology class.

September 7, 1999, John didn't sleep a wink that night. He dreamed of war with his now-ever vivid picture of men floating from the sky. Gang activity was now a citywide problem. One gang in particular loved to rob the spectators after major sporting events. Not quite sure how he would utilize his goal, John was eager to help if he could.

He now stood six feet and weighed a solid two hundred pounds. His eighteenth birthday would come in October. As he ate breakfast, the second day of school, Barbara couldn't get over how her son had grown so powerful looking. He reminded Barbara of the men she'd see on television that had Harold glued to it watching pro wrestling. "A half dozen boiled eggs, two packages of bacon," Barbara teased John, "you're going to have a heart attack."

"Oh, Mom," John said as he licked his fingers. His voice was now as heavy as Harold's. "I work out too much for the cholesterol to affect me, see? Feel these muscles." The two laughed. Seriously, Barbara asked, "Do you need any lunch money, John, or will you be okay?"

"Carolyn's treating today, Mom, but I could use some gas money." John playfully put out his hand. Barbara went to the kitchen drawer and pulled out a ten spot. "This should be enough for today."

"Thanks, Mom." Ready to head out for school, John, after finishing up in the rest room, kissed his mom good-bye for the day. Harold had business over in China and wouldn't be back for three weeks. John headed to the car garage, still remembering the punch he sustained from Williams years ago. It made John cautious, yet he was never afraid. He silently thanked his mom for saving the Coupe de Ville for him. It would come in handy for his senior year at Mount Whitney. He headed out of the garage and over to Carolyn's. John was now one of the most sought-after prep running backs in the nation; his speed at ten seconds in the hundred meters gave John an almost godlike presence in front of his peers.

Coach Al Hardy, the science teacher whose inexperience showed on the field, still had the respect of the students. He worked the kids hard during the summer so they were in excellent physical condition. Yet all the athletes were concerned about the real test—contact with other schools. Hardy took over after the first coach, Baldy Harris, died of a heart attack last season. Hardy, a small man who wore no facial hair, gave the impression of an army private at a mere observation of a stranger. The alto voice was constantly challenged by the ever-cocky youth who would wear the name Dolphin this year. "All right, guys, I want a one hundred percent effort from every one!" Hardy yelled. He then went on, "The first game is tonight. I want to prove to everyone we can still win without Baldy." The team took a respected third place last year; however, no expectations were placed on the team this year because the main core had graduated.

Hardy then excused the team from their morning classes. John, who always met Carolyn at the noon lunch hour every day, quickly went to his class after the team meeting. John's ability to stay celibate was constantly threatened by Roweeta, an African American cheerleader who wanted a chance to get John in bed. The chemistry teacher was Elizabeth Gonzales, a short stocky woman, slightly attractive but with a brilliant mind. The professor always excused athletes and cheerleaders before the big games and made no exceptions today. As she excused the members of the football team as well as the cheerleaders, John headed for the library. "No classes until noon," John thought aloud. Just then, Roweeta—who had the hourglass figure, sexy face, light complexion with no pimples, perfect teeth, and those penetrating green eyes—came up from behind John and pinched him on the butt. Instantly, John turned around to see who it was; he immediately became erect. "Hey, watch it." John casually pinched Roweeta back on the butt. All smiles, Roweeta put her arms around Cade. "Where you going, Flash?" John thought of his pulsating organ, then he sheepishly added, "From the looks of things, to a hotel." Roweeta blushed then unabashedly said, "Let's go, John." It was a seedy affair in the downtown district, yet with two horny teenagers, the only thing that mattered was privacy. John used the ten dollars Barbara had given him for gas money to pay for two hours time for renting a room. The hotel clerk, a shabbily dressed, ungroomed fellow with one good arm, hastily took the ten dollars with the promise of John bringing the other five tomorrow.

John about to explode, quickly agreed. When they made it to room 20 and unlocked the door and opened it, they were surprised at the relative cleanness of the room. The small toilet had good towels, yet there was no hot water, but the toilet worked. Roweeta cautiously pulled back the odd-smelling thin pink bedcover. No stains were on the one sheet but with the September weather like it was, she tossed the blanket to the side. John was so busy unbuttoning his shirt he almost ripped a few buttons. When John finished undressing, he watched in pleasure as Roweeta casually undressed. John, secreting now, helped Roweeta out of her blue-striped miniskirt. He almost fainted observing her in her blue panties. After kissing her lightly, John lay on the bed. For all the talk, both teens were relatively inexperienced at sex. The small talk came first, then picking it up, a surprised Roweeta had to know, "Are you a virgin, John?" John sensing he'd blow it if he lied, feebly said, "Yes, Roweeta, I am."

"Come to momma, boy," Roweeta giggled then parted her legs.

It took seemingly hours, but after checking her wristwatch, Roweeta surmised that eight minutes had passed. After sex, the two, while embracing, talked of Carolyn. Roweeta asked John, "Do you love her?" John quickly answered, "Of course I love her, she's my lifelong friend." The subject changed to Larry. Roweeta, sort of sweet on Greydog, wanted to know what John thought of him. John, not wanting rumors to spread, simply stated, "He's a lot bigger than he was at Wilburton, that's for sure."

"Well, I like him," Roweeta shot back, "but he's in some sort of gang."

"Really?" John asked. Becoming curious, he sat up in bed.

"Yes, some kind of oppressed brothers or something, and they're robbing and stealing, maybe even selling drugs." Roweeta then looked into John's eyes, smiled, then said, "Look, don't go telling anyone. You never know about Mr. Williams. He's learned a lot of tricks." She went on, "You know he majored in law, and he's going to college."

John, still stroking Roweeta's free-falling shoulder-length hair, was back in his own world—men floating from the sky. "You okay, John?" Roweeta asked. "Am I too much for you?"

"No, I'm fine, sweetheart, just thinking that's all." John, satisfied, suggested they head back to school.

The scrimmage that night against Deerfield didn't go well. The Dolphins' execution was awful. Cade ran for ninety yards on eight carries, but he was pulled early in the fourth quarter. He had managed two touchdowns on his own effort. Larry, a senior this year too, was a top prospect for a high school middle linebacker, but he didn't do well in this game. There were at least two offensive linemen waiting for his every move. With the Dolphins lacking strong defensive players, this would be a long year for the six-foot-two over two-hundred-pound all-city linebacker. Carolyn couldn't stop crying on the way home from the game. "How could you, John? You're so awful."

"Sorry, Carolyn," John said, searching for answers. "She practically threw herself on me, what was I supposed to do?" John couldn't comfort his friend, driving in the maze of traffic was difficult enough. "You could have said no!" Carolyn was furious. Roweeta had bragged all day about herself and the big star of the school having a round in a hotel. Roweeta had let it be known that John was as fast in bed as he was on the football field. John was angered at first, but with so many people patting him on the back, it only fueled his ego.

Larry, with his three-year-old son, Junior, hours after the game, felt good about completing the Naval ROTC course last year. *Now I can concentrate on joining the army reserve after graduation,* Larry pondered. Quenlin always kept the baby until 7:30 p.m., then Larry would take over until she came home. The gang was well over thirty thousand, but to Larry, they were out of control. "Damn, I'll be glad when this girl gets here. I have a meeting tonight." Terran had called the Williams's home earlier hoping to speak with Greydog. Larry now had a full beard, which he kept neatly trimmed. He had purchased a '98 Ford Taurus because of the smooth ride of the thing. The paint job was a shiny off-white affair, and this helped Larry in his decision to purchase this particular car. Quenlin didn't arrive home until eleven thirty that night. But being Friday, Larry knew Terran would wait until Saturday, knowing Larry played football that Friday night. As Quenlin entered the apartment, Larry angrily yelled, "Girl, you call next time, damn! I have important shit to do." Quenlin, used to Larry's antics now, quickly responded, "Listen, nigger, I'm home all day with this boy, so don't sass me about nothing!" Wilma, hearing the noise from her room, came to the door and yelled, "Leave my grandchild out of this argument or let me keep him!" Larry and Quenlin at the same time piped, "Okay, Ma!"

    Terran was as patient as anyone could be under the circumstances. Kank's men were idiots. The only one who made sense was the treasurer, Luke, and Terran couldn't trust him. Terran was pleased at the gang's net worth, which was over five hundred thousand dollars. Terran no longer had to use his resources, but he still had to use his vast wealth as a front for the gang. Terran didn't mind Luke's shrewd hand concerning financial matters. That Saturday morning, Terran had spent the night in his office hoping for some word from Mr. Dog; it didn't come. The small electric heater kept the room from totally freezing. As Larry knocked on Terran's door, Terran instantly knew who it was. He went to open the door. "I've been waiting for you, Mr. Dog. Everything all right?" Terran studied Larry as he asked the question. "Yes, things came up," Larry said, "but I'm okay now." Not able to help himself, Terran had to ask, "How did the game go?" A frustrated Larry let Terran know. "They wiped the floor with our ass!" Then Larry chuckled at such an ass whooping. Not understanding football, Terran could only nod his head. Terran then got down to business. "Mr. Dog, Brotherhood of the Oppressed is now a huge operation. All we can do is hope the soldiers will follow the leaders. Mr. Kank has several men he can trust. Do you need assistance from him?"

"No, man, I like things the way they are." Larry felt in control now. "Good," Terran shot back. "I have connections here in the city that will allow us to use the University of Illinois gymnasium three times a week. We can use this time to hold three meetings weekly since we have at least thirty thousand people." Terran continued, "All we want to do is keep them informed, so if need be, they can be called up to fight. Are you ready, Mr. Dog?" Larry felt this was the time to use the five percent theories he had learned from Arthur. "More than ready, T." Larry grimaced as he assured his friend.

"Good, I'll get things started with Mr. Kank," Terran stated with authority. The two shook hands and sang, "All praise to revolt!" Now smiling at each other, they parted company; they felt good about things. On his way home, Larry noticed it was well past 1:00 p.m. in the afternoon. He silently thought as he headed toward home, *All the white boys have left the gang. Now there's nothing but Mexicans and black folks. I wonder, will they accept my lecturing their ass on life?* As he pulled into the apartment complex, Larry was softly singing, "Bye, bye, Miss American Pie."

CHAPTER 9
ADULTHOOD

Both schools were cheering wildly. The strong wind, even though it had limited the air attack of both teams, didn't slow down the ground game. Homecoming for Mount Whitney didn't mean championship, but it did give the students one last glimpse of Williams and Cade. Both were topics all over Illinois. Even as the game ended, which Mount Whitney won, 21-7, no one left their seats. The cold first week in November weather seemed minimal. The school principal George Billings waited several minutes then asked for silence. Joliet Community High School had left the playing field. Billings then spoke of the two giants of Mount Whitney. "I have a special thanks for two of the greatest men to don a Dolphin uniform. Without you, we probably wouldn't not have won our seventh game. Now, we all miss Baldy; he was special. Who can forget a three-hundred-pound tall and ever-shining egg head running up and down the sidelines." The stadium roared its approval at the joke. Billings went on, "I personally want to present John Cade with this certificate of our most valuable player award, and, John, our special thanks for leading the league in rushing with over twelve hundred yards." He then turned his attention to Larry. "Mr. Williams, you too are to be thanked for your contributions. Only you could lead an otherwise undersized defensive core to ranking third in the state. It is my pleasure to award you the most improved player award!" John and Larry, for the first time ever, shook hands; both men held their tongues. Billings, a scholarly type, was short and stubby with graying hair, and he walked with a slight limp. Billings, also an ex-high school player, was teary eyed as he dismissed himself. Everyone would miss the electricity Williams and Cade brought to the table.

Harold wanted to keep John's most valuable player award certificate in his office. John wanted to keep the trophy in his ever-mounting trophy case at home in the spare bedroom. John, after going through all his scholarship letters, had turned down over twenty schools. Head coaches were coming out of the woodwork. The remaining months at Mount Whitney went rather quickly. Carolyn, who had long since forgiven John, felt guilty she didn't give in to temptation. But with John's apology and his promise to stay chaste, they mended their relationship. As the summer months approached, John surprised everyone by choosing South Carolina.

Harold and Barbara, who really wanted John at Penn State, showed their obvious disappointment. Carolyn was thrilled to leave the big city. John wanted to grow as a person outside city limits. After several heated discussions, Harold and Barbara finally gave in to John. Barbara, over dinner in early July, gave John a bug net. "Don't come crying to me when those pests attack you," she said in a playful tone. She then stroked John's thick black hair. "I won't, Mom, can you pass the peas?" John and his ferocious appetite enabled him to quickly eat his food. He didn't want to miss his personal workouts at the local gym over the summer before he and Carolyn left for South Carolina.

Larry, in the army training camp for recruits, joined so he could sharpen his warrior skills. The drill sergeant's like for Private Williams only fueled Larry's goal. The occupational skill

Larry desired was infantry. During the two odd months of training, Larry became an expert with the M16. Being taught to use the rifle professionally, Larry could now train his warriors back home in Chicago. Larry learned a new respect for the white man. He now knew one had to be very thorough to even compete in combat, let alone be able to afford supplies for a sustained effort in war against whitey. The physical training and learning how to march in formation gave Larry the discipline it took to be a soldier. After graduating from training camp in Georgia, Larry stayed over for infantry training; and after that, he would attend Chicago University on a football scholarship. His hopes were to become a reservist officer.

    Larry received a special week off from Chicago University to take care of personal business. As he stepped into the apartment, Wilma, Quenlin, and Junior were there to meet him. "Welcome home, Larry," they all yelled. They were ecstatic that Larry made it home okay. Teary eyed, Larry hugged each one of them. "I missed you all. I'm glad I'm back home." Larry looked splendid in his military green dress uniform. The cab driver carried Larry's luggage to the door; the heavy duffel bag was the last item. The boyish-looking cabby accepted his fee and quickly departed. Wilma had a large meal of sirloin steak, black-eyed peas, biscuits, and mushroom gravy. They all tore into the sumptuous meal. No one bothered speaking due to Wilma's fine cooking. Finished eating, Larry patted his stomach. "Boy, Ma, you sure know how to spoil a guy. Hell, I might go UA one day for this chow." Everyone laughed but Junior, who was busy stuffing peas into his mouth. Dying to know the meaning of chow, Quenlin asked, "What's chow?" Realizing he wasn't in training, Larry explained to his girl, "The military term for food is chow, Q." Quenlin sighed and looked deep into Larry's eyes. Observing the two, Wilma called Junior. "Come on, boy, let's go watch television. Your parents look like they want you another brother or sister."

"Stop it, Mom, you're too much." Quenlin took Larry by the hand and started leading him to the bedroom. Larry had some weight to get off his shoulders.

Terran studied the United States Army, private first class. "You look great, Mr. Dog, you ready?"

"Yes, Terran, I'm ready to get down to business." Larry looked the bill of a clean-cut all American. His military crew cut and clean-shaven face gave Larry the sophisticated look. Terran paused then explained to Larry the situation. "Mr. Kank is a sharp man, but he lacks the style, as you might say, to impress our troops. As you can see, I can't convince them, but, Mr. Dog, you certainly seem capable." Terran went on, "There will be a meeting tomorrow at the university campus at 11:00 p.m. I had to shell out good money for these rights. We will have a total of four meetings, Tuesday through Friday, ten thousand men in each meeting. They've already been informed, and each member has a specific date to be there." Realizing he was talking too much, Terran still pressed forward. "We will also have privacy. I paid for this too. The public, for now, thinks we are helping troubled youth to go straight." They both laughed at the suggestion. Terran asked, "Can you do it with your athletic and college career, Mr. Dog?" Larry, feeling like a superhuman, yelled out, "All praise to revolt!"

"Good," Terran said as he embraced Larry, then Terran prepared to close the meeting. The ten thousand men showed up. They were informed in the letter sent to them by mail to be quiet at all times. Also, they were notified to tell their parents that these meetings would be beneficial for their scholastic future. And since Larry was now in the army, they were to tell their parents that an army representative would be there doing the talking at lectures. The youth were told to inform concerned parents that the late time was due to the building being used for other activities.

Larry, not aware of perpetrators, had been warned by Kank not to put down the American way of life.

The meeting came to order at around twelve midnight. Being that time was that late, Larry figured he'd make a short speech. "Listen, men," he spoke as his voice boomed on the loud speakers. Larry studied his audience from his position on the floor of the gymnasium. He went on, "Brotherhood of the Oppressed needs trained soldiers. Now, I know you all do your exercises and train with broom handles." There was further talking, and remembering Kank's admonition, Larry went on, "You men that are capable need to enlist in the military reserve, and then you can help discipline those who can't join. Brotherhood of the Oppressed has to stay strong, and to stay strong, we need unity. One day we will be on top of the world!" Larry ended the meeting only twenty minutes later by yelling, "All praise to revolt." The youth boomed back the salute. As orderly as they came in, they filed out of the gym.

The long drive from home to Chicago didn't seem that it would be to grueling, but now that they were halfway there, John was beginning to have second thoughts. The endless strip of highway wasn't bad, but the sheer mileage seemed to wear Cade down. They made it to Tennessee. John, who had been driving over four hours, got off the expressway and headed for a local hotel. "I stayed up late last night packing and everything, Carolyn, so I'm making a stop." John said, irritated from all the driving. Carolyn, sensing the crankiness in the tone coming out of John's statement, remained silent. They arrived in downtown

Nashville at around noon that Wednesday of August. After asking seemingly one hundred people, they final found a Motel 6; and the moment John lay on the double bed in the small but neat and clean room, he snored. Carolyn turned down the volume on the television set and watched some old Westerns that were playing that day.

    By the time they arrived in South Carolina, at nine o'clock Thursday morning, John was sure he had aged ten years. Carolyn was surprised at how different the state was from the ever-busy Chicago. "John, let's take a quick tour before we check into the school, we have time." Then in her little girlie voice, Carolyn pleaded, "Please, Johnny boy?" Not able to resist the temptation, John gave in. "All right, here we go." The diversity of the state was shocking. Although they were close to Columbia, the location of the university, the old South took bites out of one's memory. Tobacco farms, people selling baskets alongside the road, and the different style of blacks, whom they noticed on the streets, were a far cry from the inner-city Negroes. After two hours of touring, John decided to head to the university. The closer they came to their new school, John began thinking of the tearful good-byes. Even Carolyn's dad, Dalton, cried, which was so unusual to John being that Mr. Jones was such a tough guy. John now felt he cheated them for not sticking closer to home. John turned off Elmwood on to the Main Street, and they both saw the university. They had to use the visitor parking space until they were registered students. A beautiful affair, and large, Carolina seemed like the perfect choice. John, as he and Carolyn got out of the car and began walking toward the visitor's center, really liked the mixture of old and new facilities; it looked splendid. Even though the weather was hot as well as humid, he and Carolyn didn't mind. They were in college at last. After getting situated, Carolyn found the dormitory, and then she and some newfound friends went on a tour of the campus. She'd promised to meet John in front of the dormitory at five o'clock that evening. John headed for the football field. Football sessions were already under way. John, a week late, still had the duties of getting a class schedule. Carolyn, whose family paid for her education, was already at home in the Deep South school. They both would probably end up doing the schedule's separately. John, who received an athletic scholarship, spent an hour getting his classes together; he majored in aircraft engineering and had a tough time getting things together. By the time he made it to the football field, John finally met the Gamecocks head coach, Verde Stratowski. Verde, probably the only man in the state who'd accepted such a low-achieving sports team, was thrilled at meeting Cade. "Well, look what we have here," Verde said in his now—Old South tongue. "If it's not the great white hope. Glad to meet you, son." The two shook hands. John then eyed the powerful shoulders of Stratowski, who had the arms of an ape. There was no weakness about the coach's physique whatsoever. "What's the matter, son, cat got your tongue?" Verde said with interest.

"No, Coach, just watching the players scrimmage." The blue eyes of Verde were the darkest John ever saw. The short but graying full head of hair gave John the impression that Coach was at least fifty. Verde blew his whistle; the shrill filled the empty stadium. "All right, men, let's hold the action. I want everyone to meet our running back, Mr. John Cade, all the way from Illinois." The team nonchalantly waved their hands. No one seemed impressed with Cade. Coach looked at his watch. "Let's take it in, men. Our first preseason is two days from now, and we don't want any freak injuries before the season starts." The Gamecocks bolted for the showers. Verde studied Cade then asked, "You all right, son? You seem like the guy who just realized he swallowed a canary." Wanting to say yes but being reasonable, John slowly answered Stratowski, "Well, Coach, the air is much cleaner here, and I'm so high on the oxygen I don't know what to say." Stratowski chuckled then politely answered John, "You'll be fine, son, I hope you're in good shape because you'll be our starter for the preseason opener against Clemson." John began feeling the butterflies that quickly popped out. "I'll be ready, Coach."

"Good." Stratowski, in his all-but-forgotten German accent, got out, "I'm counting on you to lead the team this year. We have a lot of underclassmen without much direction." John felt this would be a long four-year stay. Coach gave John the rest of the day off. "Friday you be sure and check with the athletic department, got that?"

"Gotcha, Coach." John headed back to the main campus in awe of the huge stadium of the Gamecocks. John pondered at how different college life seemed. At Wilburton, and then Mount Whitney, times were fun; but here at Carolina, one was on his own. John, away from home only one day, felt homesick already. When he and Carolyn met in front of the dormitory, the two had an evening meal together. Carolyn voiced her complaints. "Boy, John," she said bitterly, "why this school? I mean you could have gone to Southern California or even Penn State. I hate it already." John, just now beginning to bite into his double helping of meat loaf, calmed his friend. "Listen, Carolyn, if we are going to have success in our life, let's do the right things first and love our accomplishments later, just as our parents did." Sensing she'd hurt John's feelings, Carolyn perked up. "Okay, but just for you." Then jokingly, she asked, "Roweeta is not coming, is she?" John almost choked on his dinner; he laughed so hard. After the long deep look into each other's eyes, both felt they'd be fine. John ever dreaming thought of Williams and the ever-growing gang.

The long sessions began to wear on Larry. "I thought the army was tough," Larry thought as the coach ordered another drill. The linebackers for the Chicago University football team worked hard to prepare for the season. They were working on the drill called leverage for the low leverage attack. After thirty minutes of this, they switched to the door tackle. Larry was sure he would pass out with all his equipment on. When it began to rain, which was unusual for August, Larry thought it was heaven-sent. "Damn, four years of this shit and I'll be too damn tired for the pros."

Linebacker coach Thad Peters, a former player himself, who lost an eye years ago in a freak accident while he played a pickup game, released the players for the day after they had ran forty-yard sprints. Peters was going out for a short pass, but the moment he turned to catch the ball, it, being a spiral, connected right in his left eye. The damage was irreversible. After three unsuccessful surgery attempts, the eye was finally removed. The glass eye went well with Peter's rugged features. The deep, growling voice kept the players in awe of the six-five, two-hundred-pound hard-nosed coach.

After leaving the school, Larry went to the old meeting place on 103rd. As he arrived, the memories came. The rides on the Schwinn across town, which Larry still owned, always made Greydog chuckle. He never forgot Arthur; Larry promised himself not to let his mentor's death be in vain. The youths now looked up to Greydog. Each meeting, Larry would use subliminal messages. Each week, the troops would receive a letter in the mail telling them to study the material and listen for key words. It was done so as not to alert authorities, Terran's idea. This worked, for the now forty thousand members kept coming. Terran was waiting for Larry at the warehouse and ushered him inside. Comfortably seated, Terran spoke first. Now he called

Larry by his last name Mr. Williams. He began, "I want to talk to you concerning the actions of our troops. They respond to you well, and for right now, you have them cool it on their robbing neighboring cities and states after sporting events." This sombering message didn't surprise Larry. Kank and his men were cutthroats. They found ways for the youth to illegally obtain funds. According to Luke, the money the gang had accumulated had amounted to over two million bucks. Terran went on, "One day, something's going to leak and then—" Larry answered Terran. "I'll send them letters through the secretary, Terran, and then talk to them about an honest day's work." The two men laughed hard, and Larry then caught himself and explained, "Anyway, T, don't worry. We've come this far, nothing can stop us now." With his brain reaching for answers, Larry finally asked Terran the question that had been boiling in him. "What are these men doing all this for, Terran, my man?" Smiling, Terran suggested, "You'll see." That was enough for Greydog as he looked into those mysterious eyes of the ever-challenging Middle Easterner.

CHAPTER 10
THE DRAFT

The National Football League draft was over. Larry was ecstatic; he was the first player picked in the first round. Things couldn't get any better. Wilma, all smiles and tears, wouldn't stop hugging her boy. Little Larry, eight years old, didn't quite understand all the commotion, but he liked the way Quenlin kept stroking his hair. "Damn, first pick!" Larry yelled. He, over the years, had become a giant. He now stood six foot four and weighed 250 pounds. Larry never dreamed he'd go so high. The family prepared to celebrate later on, but for now, they were happy with the here and now. The Alabama Grizzlies, an expansion team in the tough Eastern Division of the National Conference desperate for someone to shore up the defense, took a chance on the volatile Williams. In college, Williams was known to blow his stack, but the Grizzlies felt he could only improve an otherwise lackadaisical defense.

As the night went on, Larry invited only close associates. He didn't want any wild partying going on at his apartment. All of Larry's former coaches called to congratulate him, but the most memorable one was Gus Thompson. Larry never admitted it, but Gus really shaped his football future. "Son, I knew you could do it," Gus said in a proud tone. "I'm proud of you, Williams, or is it Captain Williams?"

"You can call me Greydog, Coach, as my other friends do." Larry entertained Coach with his smooth way of talking. "Greydog it is." Thompson happily said, "See you on television next year, son." Gus, now teary eyed, said, "And good luck." Larry returned the salute, "Later, Coach." As he hung up the phone, Larry quickly dialed Terran's number.

The phone rang until the answering machine came on; Larry left a message informing Terran to call him.

John felt good leaving the confines of University of South Carolina for good. The Old South gave John a lesson he would never forget. John could never get over the language of some of the less-educated blacks. The Gullah language always made him chuckle. And the stories of how some people were fed to alligators in the swamps kind of frightened John. He made sure to respect the people he met there. Carolyn made sure she purchased everyone, one of the handmade baskets they picked up alongside of the road in Charleston that old black women sold there daily. Being the number six pick in the draft, John felt good about it, but he dare not entertain people and then leave them victims for the gangs now running rampant throughout Eastern America. John was sure Larry was involved with the gangs, but he couldn't pinpoint it. The Seattle Seahawks had picked John. Both he and Carolyn's family were elated at such an honor. John finished fifth in the Heisman race; he was also fourth in the nation in rushing with over fourteen hundred yards in his senior year. Yes, the year 2002 was a good year for running backs; and Cade, the fastest of all running backs, stood out with the best of them.

As the family sat in the dining room relaxing, John broke the silence by saying he wouldn't play ball this year. "What do you mean you're not playing in the league?" Harold was furious at his son. "John, you've spent years for this honor, don't blow it, son." John, ready to defend his choice, tried to calm his father. "Look, Dad, I want to spend some time in the air force reserve, and then after that, maybe I'll look into some football." Harold, thinking John may have a head injury, simply stated, "Why?" Knowing he could no longer hold it in, John explained to his father, "Look, Dad, all my life since I could remember, I've dreamed of special aircraft able to defend America's honor if need be. I want the country to benefit from my dreams, Dad." The look on John's face gave Harold the message—his son was for real. "Okay, son, but what about making a living?" John felt sheepish but not ashamed; he looked at his father and said, "Can I live here with you and Mom until I find employment, Dad?" Harold, still in love with the son he knew as the hard-nosed running back, also with Barbara pleading with him, sighed and gave in to his son.

    The Grizzlies came to terms with the top pick in the draft. Having an agent through Terran, Larry, the army reserve captain, managed to get his contract up front. A whopping ten million up front and another twenty million through long-term payments. The Grizzlies owners, although quite rich, were desperate for a superstar. They were hesitant at first, but they finally agreed to Larry's contract. With so much money, the family purchased a fine home in the Northside residential area. Larry, now relaxed about his future, was informed by Kank that there would be four meetings at the gymnasium that week. Flyers had already been sent out. Larry was asked to make a brief appearance since he was such a high-profile figure. "Don't blow our cover, G-dog, let us handle the gang, and you deal with Terran," Kank semiordered Larry at a meeting with leaders only. By now, Kank had a small army of leaders keeping the youth in line.

Before training camp for rookies opened in August, Larry had a week or so to give lectures. He now had reporters and television crews there. Larry, at a meeting, thought to himself, *Damn, I see what Kank meant.* He knew he had to really change his tune now. As he spoke, Larry was careful not to mention revolt. "Look people," Larry observed the crowd as he spoke, "you see what can be accomplished." He then emphasized the words, *through higher learning.* "I worked hard, I studied hard, and now the world is mine." The laughter let Larry know the point was taken well. After the building was silent, the curious reporters began asking questions. Larry politely answered them all without using the slogan of revolt. When the reporters left, Larry wiped the sweat off his brow. His Grizzly warm-up jumpsuit, a sleek brown affair with the Bear enigma looked splendid. His Adidas cross trainers that were especially designed for his feet matched the suit perfectly. He, Terran, and Kank, after the building had emptied, formed a semicircle. Terran spoke first, "That was a great job, Mr. Williams, you did well."

"Thanks, T." Larry was all smiles. Then Terran added, "But with things being so exposed, now we have to be careful." Kank was feeling like a leader too, but he kept his silence. He knew these two had money, and Kank learned from the streets that power and money went hand and hand. The trio whispered together, "All praise to revolt." They then departed the empty gymnasium.

Training camp was tough; Larry had been there two weeks, and he felt beat. Coach Hennard Beal, an inexperienced but cocky linebacker coach, knew that the rookies were out of shape and ordered the men to run some forty yard dashes. Larry, when his turn came, lined up. Coach blew the whistle. Larry was not a speed burner, yet he gave it all he had. At thirty yards, Larry, in full speed, felt a searing pain in his left leg, his power thrust. He went down; he tumbled over and over. Larry, knowing he had ripped up something, just lay there. He had several scrapes all over his body, which stung something awful. Hennard, sensing he'd be fired over this, ran to Larry's aid. The knee was twisted backward. Beal, a handsome muscular ex-high school gym teacher, vomited at the freak injury. A stretcher had to be brought in.

    The night after surgery, Larry had the nurses phone Terran, who came with his own doctor. They arrived in Alabama from Chicago several hours later. Larry was diagnosed as having a twisted kneecap and a torn anterior cruciate ligament. He'd be out for the season. Larry, ever-thinking, asked that Terran's physician, Dr. Akbad Moheed, be his own personal advisor. A week later, Larry informed the team that his injury was career-ending and that he would retire. At Terran's insistence, Larry had hired an attorney so the franchise couldn't file suit and renege on the contract. Finally, in and out of court settlement, two months from the accident, Larry was able to keep the upfront ten million, but the Grizzlies were free after paying Larry five million dollars over a three-year period. All sides were happy with the verdict. Back in Chicago, Larry, on crutches, would be taking it easy for a while.

    The nation, after reading the story of the sixth pick in the draft, applauded Cade. The television program *60 Minutes* aired a segment on the patriotic Cade. John spoke briefly of wanting to change America. It touched the hearts of millions. Although getting through the air force training camp was another matter. The grueling task took a concentrated effort on Cade's part. Cade had above average respect for a recruit. With his college degree, he would earn the honors of second lieutenant upon graduating. Carolyn held her own in training camp as well.

Christmas at the Cade's home was an illustrious affair. It was nearing the end of the year 2003. A good year for Cade. He and Carolyn, engaged now, happily enjoyed the holiday with their respective families at the Cade home. Harold, in a playful mood as he sipped on the spiced eggnog, prodded his son. "What about your famous craft, son, you getting things started yet?"

"In time, Dad, in time." John was more interested in observing the five-foot-high real Christmas tree purchased by Barbara from a local merchant. There were only a few presents, but this day would be special for a long time. John, a reservist jet mechanic now, couldn't wait until he had to report for duty. "Dad, with me being a reservist, what about you speaking to someone about me tinkering with commercial craft here at the airport?" Impressed, Harold said, "Good idea, son. I'll check into it, but let's celebrate for now." Then it was Carolyn's turn to share. Barbara asked, "What are you going to do in the air force, Carolyn?" Embarrassed but quickly responding, Carolyn answered, "I'm in charge of the first tactical unit supply, second lieutenant in command." Everyone laughed.

Carolyn, through sips of eggnog got out, "Hey, I majored in general studies at South Carolina, so what do you expect." The two families silently agreed with Carolyn's viewpoint. Both families then settled in to watch some Christmas specials on television before dinner was ready.

CHAPTER 11
THE TAKEOVER

Travis Air Force Base, John was upset at his commanding officer, Colonel Thomas Holden, for falling out of his chair laughing at John's idea. Finally, when John noticed Holden not smiling anymore, he spoke. "Sir, with all due respect, I think I have a fine idea." Holden finally was able to straighten himself out. He eyed his small office. The numerous awards covered a small portion of the meticulous blue room. Except for the family portrait and large plaque with his rank insignia and name on it, Holden kept a typical room for a high-ranking officer, bare with only essentials for decorations. "That may be, Lieutenant Cade, but, son, do you know what you're asking? Just to get something like that started would take possibly billions of taxpayers' dollars." Then sighing, Holden, a tall man with a square jawline, a high forehead and a gumdrop nose, had the perfect voice for authority—a rich baritone that was a booming attention grabber. Holden tried to talk some sense into John. "With your respect you already have, son, why not let the local authorities handle the problem of gangs?" Not convinced, John thanked the colonel and requested to speak to a higher command. Colonel Holden, then shaking his head, granted John's request. Being that it was Monday and John was flying back to Chicago in a few days, he telephoned his dad, hoping that he would be at home. "Hello, who's speaking?"

"Hi, Dad, this is John. Hey, look, Dad, could you possibly get a hold of the city mayor and a few politicians to look at my idea? I'm having problems getting my point across to my commanding officer." Concerned, Harold felt he had to use his weight. "Let me make a few phone calls, son, we'll get something done. Get back to me tomorrow." Relieved, John thanked his father. The two hang up their respective phones. Harold quickly got on the phone. His brief talk with Mayor Daley went well. He was told to call a local politician who had connections in the White House. Five hours later, 11:00 p.m., Harold was called. The message had been put through, an air force major general got the request; he told Harold he'd be pleased to look over young Lieutenant Cade's idea. Harold called John at the base the next morning. John, playing the waiting game, received word that he had a long distance call. Cade rushed to the phone in the duty officers' quarters. "Lieutenant Cade here!" he said excitedly.

"John." It was Harold over the phone. "When can you get here in Chicago?" Harold asked. John answered, "By the end of next week, Dad, why?" Harold then informed John that an air force general received the idea, but he wanted John to use the proper chain of command in order to meet him. John was barely able to contain himself. "I'll be there by Friday, Dad. I have a weekend pass, and because of a special assignment, I can't leave right away." Then John added, "I'll be sure and use the chain of command."

"Great," Harold said. "See you then, son."

The air force general, Ty Wong, an American Chinese who was born in the States, talked to some local politicians about young Cade's plans. They all were curious about looking over the idea. A special meeting was set up that Saturday, January 8, 2004, at the naval yard in Chicago. General Wong represented the air force from the headquarters in Washington DC. Second Lieutenant Cade brought his blueprints along. General Wong, a small quick man with the typical slant of eyes, yet fit and trim, rose through the officer rank quickly. He'd only been in the air force for twenty tears, yet his knowledge of several languages helped him rapidly advance in his career in the air force. General Wong looked over the blueprints. "Lieutenant Cade," the general said, "I myself like this idea, but we need approval of my people in DC."

Cade gave the expected answer, "Yes, sir!" After only an hour, the meeting came to an end. The secretary of defense held a private meeting. It was then up to Congress to approve the craft that would be called G-Strings.

Four months had passed without a word. John had a job as a jet mechanic for Chicago's O'Hare Airport. Carolyn began a life as a homemaker. She felt that soon, she and John would tie the knot, so she didn't want every available man looking up her skirt. John, still residing at home with his parents, was relaxing after a hard day's work in the middle of May. With the weather warming up, it was a welcome relief. John was now a supervisor of jet engineers. As he lay back, Barbara notified John that he had a phone call. "Thanks, Mom." "Hello, John Cade speaking."

"Hello, John, this is Jarred Mount, Department of Defense, speaking," John's heart raced. He quickly sat up in bed and answered, "Yes, sir!"

"Son, we are impressed with your idea, and from the looks of things, the government will fund the project. By the way, Lieutenant, you will be receiving a substantial amount of money once the construction of the G-Strings get under way." John, thinking the worst, was completely turned around by this turn of events. He answered, "I don't know what to say, sir."

"Don't say anything, son, that would be best. Let the public be the last to know." Mount then abruptly hung up the receiver, then a female voice just as quickly came on the line. "Sir, give us your name, rank, and serial number and current address. You'll receive payment in two weeks."

"Yes, ma'am," Cade quickly replied. Two years later, under air force supervision, Boeing had completed six thousand of the miniature jets. Special hangers were built at the old Edwards Air Force Base near the Mojave Desert in California. Twenty huge, over a mile in width and a half of a mile in length, metal-framed hangers housed the weapons of war.

The test flights on several of the aircraft went well. Although landing them proved difficult due to size, they really shook at first touch after being airborne.

After his four-year reservist stint, Larry received his honorable discharge. An army captain now, trained in the art of infantry, and with millions at his disposal, Greydog now felt he could talk the talk with the best of them. He and Terran had complete respect of the gang. The friends Terran began introducing to Larry were anti-American types. With Kank keeping things in check back in Chicago, everybody was happy now. Terran, making a trip to Alameda by himself, got a chance to talk to some people from his part of the world. Terran also met with Frarard, his longtime associate from Iraq at the Oakland International Airport. They quickly greeted and left the crowded air travel department and went to Frarard's home in East Palo Alto. Terran loved the easygoing style of California. Compared to Chicago, the weather sure was comfortable. Frarard, middle-aged, stocky, and plain looking for an Easterner, spoke with the same accent as Terran; but being that Frarard had been in the United States for so long, he had a much bigger vocabulary than Terran. "So how's the operation, Terran?" Frarard asked curiously. "So far so good," Terran said as he studied the small home. No pictures in the living room, just copies of the *Wall Street Journal* lying around the kitchen floor. "I think we are ready to come to California," Terran nervously said to the dangerous Frarard. Frarard then reprimanded his friend in a corrective tone, "Don't think, you must be sure. The American authorities will not hesitate to wipe you out, even if they suspected foul play, got it?"

"We are sure, boss, I have been training men for some ten years. If they don't run away, we will keep the law at bay long enough to get the nuclear warheads through so we can transport them by truck to the designated location." Frarard was pleased.

"Good, good, now you pay each man one thousand dollars and get them out here in California. We can begin the takeover in two months." The two prepared for dinner. Later that night when Terran arrived in Chicago, he phoned Kank to pick him up. On time, Kank quickly ushered Terran out of the notorious airport. On the way to the warehouse on 103rd, Terran questioned Kank. "Are your men ready, Mr. Kank?"

"Hell yes," Kank shot back. "My people stay ready." Terran then asked, "What about your leaders?" Terran wanted to be sure.

"Man, all my men are ready." Kank began to get frustrated at the foreigner. "What's this all about, Terran?"

"We are ready for a takeover, Mr. Kank, and I want you to be ready. We have a thousand dollars for each man to make the trip, and if they are successful, there may be more money for them." Kank took his eyes off the road to look at Terran and almost crashed. Straightening the vehicle, Kank said, "Damn!

Man, that's a lot of money. That will put a big dent in our treasure." Terran, who knew things were in his palm now, requested that Kank buy used cars and get Luke into renting at least eight thousand buses. "Damn, Tee, what's on your mind? Whew, shit." Kank felt he was out of his league. Terran calmed his friend. "Mr. Kank, the men will board buses from at least one hundred different locations throughout the Eastern part of America over a three-month period." When they arrived at the warehouse, Kank felt relieved, but he knew he had a lot of work to do. "I'll see you in two weeks, Mr. Kank." Terran then exited the vehicle and waved as Kank drove away. Terran wanted no one to know where he lived.

Even though he was viewed as the leader, Larry felt he wasn't calling the shots, but he remembered Arthur's dream. Relaxing at home with his family late Friday night, Larry received a phone call; it was Kank. "Greydog, shit is getting ready, man. In the next couple of months, we are going to hit it, you ready?" Since his family was there, Larry kept his cool. The October rain fell against the windowpane; the wind was frisky tonight. Larry, now relishing being a multimillionaire, began having second thoughts about the gang until Arthur popped in his mind. "All praise to revolt," Larry said after a few proddings from Kank. "I'm ready." Kank then bid his farewell but not before informing Greydog to meet him at 7:30 p.m., Saturday, at the warehouse for a discussion.

That Saturday night on 103rd, a meeting was held for revolt leaders. Terran, looking over the men, trembled at the ferocity of them. Kank had roll-called and then went to Gummy Bear. "You ready to enforce things, Gummy?" In a voice that resembled a bear and a body that looked like one, Gummy answered, "Shit man, I've been waiting at least eight years, what do you mean ready? Let's go." The other men received orders;

Luke was asked how much money was available. "I see us holding six million we can get a hold of instantly, the other five we have to use bonds."

"Good," Kank said, and then he told Luke to get on the phone during the next few days and get hold of travel agencies to charter buses and several thousand air line tickets, all to be done in the next thirty days. "I'll need help," Luke said, not hiding the sarcasm. Kank with Terran's permission got Slayer Sandstone to help out Luke with the life-sucking assignment. Slayer, considered next in line to Kank in authority, grumbled his approval. Slayer, also known as Philip Harper, almost made it to the professional ranks of the hardwood, but he couldn't control his temper. Slayer stood tall among the men. At six foot six, he commanded respect. Originally from St. Louis, the mean streets taught Slayer the art of survival. Terran told the men how to handle the authorities. "Tell them it's a program for the disadvantaged youth to visit California. The program will be called Save the Youth." The hardy laughter from the men caused Terran to really howl; it sounded silly to him, grown men laughing that way. More serious now, Terran asked for the meeting to adjourn. Each man sang out, "All praise to revolt!" The building quickly emptied except for Terran and Greydog.

They waited for everyone to leave. Terran spoke first. "What do you think, friend?" Larry, feeling a little better about the situation, eyed his friend who had aged over the years. "I'm ready, T, but I feel awful about leaving my family behind." Terran, knowing this was Larry's chance to back out, observed the huge black American. "You'll do fine, my friend, just stay behind the scenes." Both men, after Terran had locked the doors, went their separate ways.

The men received their letters throughout the coming days, with the thousand-dollar checks and letter assignment as to where to go to board the buses. Terran was good to the men, who felt loyal to the gang. The specially picked men that would operate the abandoned army base near Oakland would drive the several hundred used cars that were purchased by Slayer and Luke to California. Once there, they would have the food and supplies waiting for the rest of the troops, the forty-eight thousand hardened young toughs of Chicago. Two months passed, the traveling across the country went well considering that there were many people. Four youths were killed when a tire blew out near Arizona, but they weren't missed. No one even bothered to claim the bodies, but when police found a letter that didn't burn in the crash, they notified Chicago police.

The police in Chicago notified Larry, who hadn't left the city yet. Larry, feeling the heat, explained the letter, yet the police weren't buying the story. Chief Alto Wilson, a black American, felt something was strange about men being informed to revolt, never mind Larry's story of a secret password. Wilson, a narrow-minded man with a deep hatred for criminals, slit his eyes when he warned Williams of a possible arrest. He then slammed the phone down. A small man with a pinhead and a birdlike face, with a permanent frown, he remembered the streets well. Street blacks to him were people who didn't use their potential positively. Wilson cursed himself as he phoned Oakland police. Wilton wanted to put a stop to things. Larry, knowing he had to warn revolt, drove his old vehicle, a 1999 Lincoln Navigator over to Lobeam's house. "Look, Lobeam, call Terran and tell him the police is on to us." Larry quickly left before anyone could follow him. Lobeam didn't get involved with the revolt, but since his phone wasn't bugged, he'd help out with the communication of the revolt. Larry then went to his home, and he told everyone to pack a suitcase apiece; they would take a trip soon.

The men, all restless now, were uplifted when twenty semitrucks arrived. No one was surprised that the weapons were aboard the trucks. With Frarard using the army base as a shelter, the gang had a place to rest their heads. His paying the California government the fee of five million dollars to operate the base for one month didn't stir any suspicion yet. Food supplies were already taken care of by Frarard. The trucks were quickly unloaded with the help of forklifts and then stored in the old armory of the base. The Oakland police took Wilson's warning haphazardly; no way would they see this as much of a problem. But they promised to keep their eyes open. California law also prohibited them to react irrationally about the situation. The youth, with just enough room to sleep aboard the base, ate one meal a day for one week. On December 1, Wednesday, one month away from 2006, Frarard felt this was as good a time as any. He ordered Terran to hold a meeting and then arm the young soldiers. Each man listened intently as they were instructed over the loudspeakers, "Come and receive your weapons." Anxious young men quickly grabbed the AK-47 assault rifles. Five hundred Russian-made light-shoulder bazookas were handed out. There were two hundred Jeeps available. *The grail and blowpipes would come in handy,* Frarard thought. With each man having one thousand rounds apiece, they were ordered to take over Alameda County, the central island near Oakland. The main island, which covered six miles, would be perfect to take over, but they only wanted the residential area. The ever-thinking Frarard had one hundred older banged-up school buses that were still in shape enough to shuttle the men from the old army base. The shuttle of buses at eleven thirty that Monday night went smoothly. As the first five thousand men with weapons at the ready descended on the Bay Area county, concerned homeowners began calling the police. The Oakland Police Department, now at full alert, checked on the situation, sending twenty units. Officers William Parker and Stanley Bean were the first police to arrive at the scene. They couldn't believe their eyes. Both men saw possibly thousands of armed men converging on homeowners. As Parker, the senior officer of the two, called for backup, someone targeted him with a blowpipe. As the officer excitedly yelled over his radio, "Possible terrorist take over!" Their lives went up in an oblivion of flames along with the patrol car. The other officers began firing at the large group. With traffic being light, it only heightened the shoot-out.

The gang, ruthless, was feeling unstoppable. The buses continuously shuttled men in. The gang mercilessly fired at the twenty units. After five minutes, the firing stopped. Forty officers lay dead. The Brotherhood of the Oppressed began running the people who lived in the area out of their homes. People were frantic as they were told take only their cars. After killing the policemen, the oppressed knew they would die, yet no one cared. The chance of taking a city somehow excited them.

An alarmed mayor of Oakland, Thornton Jackson, on his first term, wouldn't send more units. He, for now, would play the waiting game.

Terran and Frarard stayed put on the army base until it emptied. Afterward, they headed to San Leandro Bay to wait for the small ship with the nuclear warheads, which was to arrive shortly after the takeover.

Over forty thousand armed youth now patrolled the residential area of Alameda. Emergency news flashed on television throughout Northern California. Alarmed citizens wanted something done. With the deaths of the officers, a special unit was called in to talk to the leaders of the gang. Kank, with bullhorn in hand, talked to the special officers who were in an armored vehicle. Captain Jorga Rodrigues, a fourteen-year veteran on a special task assignment, pleaded through the armored vehicle to let them remove the corpse of the slain officers. Kank, who knew that the youth were firing at their own discretion, yelled at Rodrigues, "Do it at your own risk!" Then, thinking over the matter, Kank informed his leaders through the portable radio not to fire. The bodies were quickly removed. The coroner's vehicles, with the armored vehicle, finally left the area.

Larry, in Georgia, now thanked the stars he'd changed his mind about going to California. He knew they couldn't pin anything on him, but a low profile was a must.

California governor, the Honorable Kelvin Bryant, on his second term as governor, was too young to be in such a lofty position. At thirty-seven years of age, his degree in law at the University of Southern California didn't prepare him for such an emergency. Bryant had not held office before winning the election. Blonde and heavyset, Bryant could win just about anyone over with his sharp and trustworthy personality. He went to his advisors in a special meeting. "I'm at a crossroad, gentlemen, the National Guard or sheriff deputies?" After a two-hour briefing, the army sent in its reservist ground force of twelve thousand men. The armed guardsmen had to be called to special duty. Their job was to hem the gang members in with only the San Francisco Bay behind them. It took two days for the men to be ready. After a serious pat on the back from the governor, and backup from the Sheriff department, the guardsmen moved in.

The gang lookout, near the bridge connecting Alameda to Oakland, radioed back to Kank that army troops were headed their way. With members of the oppressed using homes as shields, they were waiting. As the army troops neared the bridge separating Alameda from Oakland, a huge blast erupted, damaging the bridge. The remaining guardsmen trucks were divided, some used the tunnel connecting Alameda to Oakland, whereas the rest of them had to go around and use the ramp off express 88. The members of the oppressed were enjoying themselves now as they had access to a whole city. Things looked great for now. Two hours later, the guardsmen confronted the troops again. The twenty or so thousand oppressed members covering that side of the area fired away at the oncoming vehicles. The guardsmen began firing back. Everyone was taking cover; the oppressed then began firing bazooka rounds at the guardsmen's vehicles, and several hundred guardsmen were lost. Saving ammunition now on their minds, the oppressed ceased firing and began to wait for another onslaught from the authorities.

The governor pulled the guardsmen back. He decided to wait two weeks before sending in more troops. The governor knew food would be a heavy weight for the oppressed to bear knowing they would run out in the near future.

Mayor Thornton Jackson pleaded with Alameda and Oakland residents to stay calm, and that things were under control. Telephone calls were swamping the city. Some homeowners who lived near the takeover began arming themselves; no one felt safe.

The small ship containing the six nuclear warheads arrived via Pacific Ocean and on through the San Francisco Bay. The ship called the Tiny Merchant in American language was able to avoid being searched by the Coast Guard or United States Customs by sheer good fortune. The ship anchored two hundred yards from the shore. The six-foot-high triangular-shaped cones would then be moved to a yacht.

It was Saturday, December 7, all was well according to the plan of the Middle Easterners. The men Terran hired were as quick as possible at getting the warheads on the ship. Two feet in width, the cones had to be delivered two at a time. It was a frightening move for the terrorist to get the cones on the deck of the yacht, but finally the cones were on land, waiting to be shipped by vehicle. The tractor-trailer rig waited to be loaded. Its destination would be Los Angeles, California. The trailer was outfitted with the slogan Cal's Produce for cover. The warheads, which were deactivated for the moment, were loaded up front, then the lettuce would be loaded behind them, perfectly covering the cones. The driver of the rig, Haseen Qualif, a small thin man with a crew cut, who spoke English just enough to qualify for driving trucks, drove the rig toward the Oakland Bay Bridge.

CHAPTER 12
SEND IN THE MARINES

The leader of the gang was Kank now. Kank, realizing Terran was nowhere to be found, became suspicious of the funny-talking so-called revolt leader. "Son of a bitch has set our asses up. That's all right, we will fight our way out of this shit." Kank had a handful of leaders who had their own personal radiomen. He informed them to watch the food supplies because the situation could get funky. Slayer Sandstone radioed Kank back. "Kank, how many people have we lost so far? I've checked, and it looks like food will get scarce in another week in my estimation." Kank, still confident, ordered all stores and markets in the vicinity to be looted. "Whoever is close to food, Slayer, have them take it." He then answered Slayer's question. "I stopped counting at four hundred, Slayer Stone, anyway they have piled the dead ones near the beach. We can't do anything else." The two men went over strategies on the radio with those who had them. The other forty odd thousand waited for instructions.

One week later, Christmas Day was only twelve days away, and Governor Bryant received a phone call from the president, Simon Montgomery. "Hello, Mr. Bryant," the president was fond of the young governor. "How's the war?"

"Fine, sir, we are going to starve them out," Bryant answered. The answer didn't sit well with Montgomery. "Listen, son, by Christmas Day, we want that riffraff out of California, or I will be forced to play my hand, that clear, Bryant!" Governor Bryant with no other alternative called the big boss's bluff. "Look, sir, I don't want to lose any more men. We've lost near three hundred, so what I'm going to do is starve them out." Montgomery, on his first term, and had earned the office with sheer will, was annoyed with California's headman. A Vietnam veteran, who served in the Coast Guard, Montgomery was as tough as they came. Over six foot and a tick over seventy, Simon feared no man. His experience as a prizefighter during his youth made Montgomery a popular choice of the people. Having compassion on Bryant's plan, the president then ordered the governor, "You keep them hemmed up, Bryant, and I'll get back to you."

The president, after going over the situation with Congress and Department of Defense, had no other alternative but to try the new aircrafts that were just sitting in the desert, waiting to be used. After careful consideration, the president decided only one branch would be able to pinpoint targets with effective precision. With time ticking away, Montgomery would let experienced air force pilots man the aircrafts; but at his orders, marines would mount the gun seats.

December 21, the marines of First Marine Division were put on standby, president's orders. The marines knew of the crises in Oakland, yet without orders, their hands were tied. The huge training facility near Oceanside, California, was home to over eighteen thousand Leathernecks, the famed name coming from marines of old who fought with leather around the back of the neck for protection while engaged in combat. Six thousand marines were told to "have your gear packed. We are moving out December 23." The excited marines had no clue as to what kind of assault would take place, but the corps taught one to be ready for anything.

General Winston Althurst, a marine of thirty years, was now commandant of the corps, a position he relished. Althurst, from deep Georgia, knew what pressure America could put on a young heart. Every year, his Marine Corps spent hours straightening out young men who, after two decades of civilian life, had become soft. Althurst realized that somehow, these gang members had lost hope in securing a home, a decent wife, and a good living. Now the president had no other recourse but to snuff out their young lives. Althurst was a burly man with ice-blue eyes and a limp from a piece of shrapnel during the Invasion of Grenada, when he wore the bars of lieutenant colonel. Althurst couldn't help but shed a tear as he gruffly thought to himself, *Maybe there was some damn fine material lost in that crowd of idiots.* He then turned his attention to the plethora of lower-ranking officers prepared to take notes during the president's instructions concerning the invasion. Everyone in the briefing room was shocked that the president would use the G-Strings. The new craft had only been used for test runs. The Strings hadn't flown actual combat missions. "Gentlemen," Simon barked over the loudspeakers in the war room, "we have a crisis. Now, we have never, since the Civil War, been faced with shedding blood of fellow Americans on American soil. Yet this takeover of a prominent city in one of the states of the Union gives us no other alternative but to take back our streets. With this maneuver, which we'll call operation G-force, I want a full report on the activities of our men. We may have to utilize this tactic on a future date." Cameras were flashing rapidly, yet the public wasn't to know until the first strike.

Terran had phoned Lobeam long distance. Terran was now in the Philippines. He informed the news carrier to get Williams a message to get out of America. Lobeam spent hours trying to reach Greydog. Finally, through Wilma's brother, he got Larry's phone number in Savannah. "Look, Greydog," Lobeam patiently got out, "I have a message for you: get to the Philippines, Luzon to be correct, someone will meet you at the airport in Manila. See you later, Greydog." Then Lobeam, who was paid handsomely for this work, hung up the telephone.

Larry, worried now, knew he was in some deep shit. With Wilma having enough currency to last for years, Larry's main objective was to have the strength to leave Quenlin and little Larry here in the States. Quenlin had blossomed into a beautiful young woman. She could more than hold her own in the dating game, but Larry had grown to love her. Still he knew staying in America, he'd be a sitting duck. He finally, after hours of contemplation, decided to give Quenlin a substantial amount of funds to tide her over. Larry, while giving her the check, made up a story. "Look, Q, I have some business to take care of, but I'll be back." She took the news well, better than Larry figured she would. "It's okay, Larry, I'll manage. Little Larry and I will be fine." Junior however didn't take it so well. "I want to go, Daddy," he cried, grabbing Larry's leg in the process. It tugged at Larry's heart, yet he had to leave his son. "Maybe next time, okay, little man," Larry said teary eyed as he held his son, possibly for the last time. With Terran already talking Larry into putting money in an overseas account in Switzerland, he didn't worry about his financial dealings. After packing two suitcases, Larry phoned a cab.

December 23, Friday, 0400 hours, the last one thousand marines who had been transported earlier got their respective field beds together. As the rest of the marines arrived and settled in, formation was called. In charge of the operation was Colonel Jake Brand, an eighteen-year veteran of the corps. Brand had never been to war, but the rugged conditions of being a marine prepared him well. Brand, a medium-built under six foot, forty-two-year-old officer had seen his share of young men in and out of active duty service on behalf of the corps. With his degree in communications, the quick-witted Brand could talk sense in to any man. As the marines broke down to their perspective units, formation was called. Brand had center stage of over six thousand young marines. Brand eyed the eager combatants then gave instructions, "Listen up, Marines, Major General Hector Gonzales is flying in from headquarters DC and will quickly brief us about our mission." The colonel began informing the marines about personal hygiene while in the field; then out of nowhere came the Huey helicopter, which had landed a good four hundred yards away from the troops. Sand flew everywhere.

The general waited for the dust to clear before he unboarded. The marines stood at rigid attention while waiting for instructions. Edwards Air Base, which had been closed for at least a decade, was now in use for special assignments. As the general came closer to the marines, he eyed them quickly. After a salute from Brand, who afterward took his position in formation, Gonzales spoke. Gonzales, a short and stocky Spaniard with a menacing personality, was a career marine all the way. Gonzales's eyes went from left to right as he spoke in the typical Mexican accent. "This is not a game, gentlemen, what we have here is a national crises. These poor misinformed individuals think they can walk all over God's green earth without obeying the civilian authorities. That's where we come in, Marines, to let the country know we will enforce the law." Gonzales went on, "Now, we all understand this is a domestic enemy, Marines. Yes, they are American citizens, gentlemen, but they have been poisoned. Word to the wise, Marines, keep your ears open because the air force will fly these miniature assault craft, and we don't want any miscommunication, Marines. Thank Lieutenant Cade of the air force, gentlemen, otherwise you'd be paratroopers, and Uncle Sam doesn't want to waste his good men, so dammit, Marines, he gave us steel balls!" Gonzales's motivating speech received the marine war cry, "uuraah!" The general went on, "Instructions are to shoot for targets, Marines. We want to save valuable property if need be." Gonzales then departed, leaving no doubt that the corps meant business. That evening, excitement could be heard all over the Edwards facility. There were nervous airmen running errands. Young marines, anxious to prove to everyone that they were still the finest fighting force on whatever level, enjoyed the free time. At 0600 hours, formation was held after an early chow in the several dozen field mess halls. One could feel the professionalism as the marines, bodies locked, stood ready. Colonel Brand told the young warriors of their assignment this morning. The lonely stretches of desert were plainly visible.

Coyotes howled in the distance, and a few jackrabbits scurried to get to their burrows.

The test runs in the G-Strings would be held today. The air force had already tested the Strings, so they knew the craft could be tricky; they warned the marines what to do in a possible crash. There were doubts about the stability of the jets once they were fully weighed down with gear, weapons, and men. The G-Strings were sixteen feet in length. The front end of the String was slender, one-foot wide at the nose and widened to form the triangular-shaped design of the craft; its width went from one to eight feet. The Strings had two three-foot-wide wings. The wheels were borrowed from large engine motorcycles, one guide wheel in front, one foot from the nose of the String, and two rear wheels that were positioned perfectly on each side to balance the craft for takeoff. This gave the String the height of four feet, including the inside of the ship, which had three feet worth of titanium steel alloy, three inches thick all around, and rounded at the sides. The String resembled a triangle go-cart, yet the two-inch bulletproof two-feet-high cover with multilayered laminated glass made it clear, this craft was for real. At the bottom part of the String was the power thrust, which complicated things a little bit. The miniaturized turbo jets with jet nozzles in the rear of the craft formed the power thrust. Due to size, the String only had a fifty-mile radius. The three-feet-a-piece wings on both sides were for steering maneuverability and also to house fuel. The insides of the String were all business. With Cade's direction, the 5.56-millimeter rounds from the famed M16 would arm the cannons. The two middlemen and the rear shooter with the rotating chair gave the String's firing positions. Each mount, when fully loaded, carried five hundred rounds. With the aid of technology, each craft had two specially designed small heat-seeking interceptors. They would help in the event of the enemy using antiaircraft missiles. The tiny cockpit and flying instruments were all that resembled the metal birds of war that were usually used to disassemble lives. The instrument panel had the components of its larger brother. From the cat-eye system to the magnesym remote compass components. Also included was the high precision clock. The cabin pressure altitude indicator was intact as well. The marines and pilots did have to wear MC-4 partial pressure suits while operating the Strings for safety reasons. At 1300 hours, December 24, the test runs were ready. Thirty marines were chosen out of First Marine Division. The marines got a kick out of positioning themselves inside the String. The dark blue paint job with the yellow-colored numbers really stood out on the Strings. Aboard craft X7029, Corporal Allen Peterson was thrilled at the infrared glasses and specially designed earmuffs that were to be worn at all times during flight. "We'll probably see a lot of naked women through their windows," he remarked. "Well, Marine, when those bastard underworld characters see this craft coming at them, they will be desperate. Don't let your tool take you to dead-man school, stay alert." Captain Maxwell of the Fifteenth Air Force reminded his passengers that this was no cakewalk. "We'll be fine, sir, if not we will regroup in hell!" Peterson barked, "Have it your way, son." Maxwell politely sighed at the tough remark of the young marine.

Today would be a dry run. The Strings would one by one make touch-and-go landings. Once airborne, the marines would be allowed rapid and slow fire at various targets on the desert floor. As the ten Strings ascended, the cheers were deafening. The miniature jet had tremendous control and versatility; it was a success.

During the last maneuvers, String X129 somehow misdirected a turn just as X708 was turning wide; there was no avoiding contact. The explosion filled the sky. Terrified airmen and marines could see parts of both human and jet falling from the sky. The emergency crews went quickly to the scene. The flight experiment, although a success, was called off for the day. Brand and company held a brief ceremony for their fallen comrades. The specially designed miniature parachutes weren't needed this time. That night, despite the crash, marines were optimistic about the exercise. Sergeant Leroy Daniels, who had been in the corps for twelve years, couldn't stop talking. He went from tent to tent with episodes of how he would thrash gang members. Daniels was a bit defensive about things, being that he knew the gang was of minority origin. Finally in the noncommissioned officers' tent, Daniels was silenced as a gruff voice commented in the dark, "Come off it, Daniels, let me get some rest. If it weren't for the corps, you'd be one of those misfits." This brought a chorus of laughter. Not being able to see who said it, Daniels angrily went to his quarters. "Screw the assholes," Daniels said dejectedly. "They just don't know a good story when they hear it." Daniels, a scrappy medium-built dark green marine, had paid his dues to be called sergeant. The years of toil more than provided him with leadership bestowed on each individual who wore three stripes, not to mention the crossing rifles.

Early wake-up was called At 0100 hours, Sunday morning. While the rest of America nervously celebrated Christmas, the marines and air force had business to take care of. Chow, a special breakfast of steak and eggs, went quickly. The first wave of nine hundred marines were told to prepare themselves. The other waves of combatants were told to stand by and wait for orders. The weather, being only twenty-two degrees above zero, didn't faze the troops. The anxious marines wanted nothing better than to put a stop to the madness.

The air force briefed its three hundred pilots who were on the first wave of the first team. Major General Howard Keaton was miffed that airmen weren't the shooters, yet he wasn't too upset about it being marines behind the cannons. The general observed his pilots; he then quickly briefed them. "People, we are going to do a lot of strafing this morning to pull the element out. With our surveillance cameras in the sky, we determined that these people are very low on supplies. They've been holed up a little over three weeks. Now, orders from higher authority want as many survivors as possible. We want to know who organized the enemy." The general added one more thing, "Also, men, we don't want to destroy valuable property if at all possible. You've been briefed, men!" Keaton, known for his antics in Vietnam while a pilot, left the officers' tent and headed for his own vehicle. He would then be briefed himself by the secretary of defense over lunch later that day. As he slid his large solid frame into the backseat of the all-terrain vehicle, an airman, walking by, locked his body and saluted the graying yet youthful-looking Keaton who, even though the salute wasn't required, returned the salute! "Let's ride, gentlemen," he ordered the driver who then led the motorcade out of the desert.

CHAPTER 13
G-STRINGS

It was 0500 hours, Christmas morning. The G-Strings of the first wave were driven aboard the C-5A Galaxy transports that were redesigned to off-load the Strings from the sky. Each Galaxy held ten Strings. The operation was huge, yet Uncle Sam spared no cost. This would determine whether the Strings could be used in future catastrophes. The one hundred Galaxies with jet assist would fly the Strings high above the target then release them through the specially designed rear hatch. With each man set, the first wave headed to Oakland. The air-traffic controllers guided the huge craft into the sky; the sound was ear shattering.

The gang felt odd that they still had water and electricity. The members were on serious food rations, one meal a day but plenty of water. Everyone was a nervous wreck waiting on action. Kank, Slayer, and Gummie Bear now had their own dwelling place to hole up in a simple one-story, three-bedroom home facing the bay, but it served its purpose. Kank, the quick thinker and always ahead of himself, let his comrades hear some of his thoughts. "With this many armed people, man, I was sure they would cut off the juice and water." Gummie, who had hell with the forced diet, spoke his view, "Man, if they did, I would have left this shit a long time ago, probably surrendered." The trio laughed. Silently, they knew they would leave in body bags. Slayer, ever slick, pulled out some weed. "I have been saving this shit. It's early in the morning, but it will go down good with this Crown Royal I found in one of the drawers in one of the bedrooms. Whoever lived here sure made good use of things." The men all nodded in agreement. Slayer rolled up a cigarette, quickly lit it, and passed it to Gummie. Slayer began to drink the liquor; it burned hard going down. "Whew, that felt good," Slayer said as he passed the liquor around also. Gummie, angry that he was trapped in this war, spoke out, "How in the hell did we get trapped in this shit anyway, Kank?" Kank finally spilled the beans, "That damn Terran promised me wealth, man, plus we were making a killing off those young fools when the robbing and stealing was going on. Hell, you know that, Gummie, I made two hundred thousand just off the interest of the bank account." Gummie, who did not make as much off the foolish teenagers but was still able to give his family at least eighty thousand over the years, voiced his opinion, "I can't complain either, Kank, I just hate to die for it." Slayer finally spoke, and the effects of the booze and weed made him think clearer. "Man, while these fools are still sleeping . . ." He checked the time, 5:14 a.m. This rang a bell in the three men head, for they all looked at each other and nodded their heads. Slayer took the last hit on the weed, smashed the butt on the scarcely worn beige carpet, and peeked outside; no one stirred. They took the old army Jeep, which was full of bullet holes, out of the driveway of the home and pushed it away from the other homes. A half mile down the road, the three men jumped in the vehicle and tried to start it; the vehicle sputtered to life. They were no more than a half mile down the road when they were stopped by guardsmen. The three were roughly thrown out of the vehicle. They were taken to police headquarters where they were detained.

The remaining gang members could get no answer from Kank's hideout. Finally, Wobbly decided he'd check on things.

Wobbly drove his Jeep down to the modest white, stucco-coated home. Once there, he saw the door wide open. As he got out of the Jeep and went inside the place, he found the residence empty. Wobbly got on the radio to Specks, who was waiting for a reply. Through static, Specks heard Wobbly, "It's empty, man, and their rifles are still here, and the Jeep is missing." Specks, an above-literate man, knew Kank and company wouldn't last long with the authorities. "Don't worry, Wobbly, being that we killed police and guardsmen, they won't last long. Get the food you can and get back here, man." Before Wobbly could reply, a loud *whoosh whoosh whoosh* came from overhead. "All to be damned," Specks yelled, "they are coming from the sky!" Then he hollered, "Get the bazooka men ready!" The rest of the gang members, fully awake now, scrambled outside with their weapons firing blindly at the G-Strings. The cold December air didn't faze the oppressed. The second wave of Strings filtered from the sky. Several dozen oppressed were ripped open by strafe fire; this angered the gang who were now cursing openly and loudly as they fought back.

The marines, picking their targets, came in on a third wave. With the blowpipes handy, the gang fired a dozen projectiles in the direction of the Strings. The missile interceptors worked beautifully; the explosions rocked the morning air. Oakland television crews raced to be as close as possible to the scene. They relayed the message to the shocked public. Civilians, not knowing what to do, silently thanked God for the intervention. Terran's army of some six hundred men, who posed as fishermen, came in from the San Francisco Bay. They brought food and ammunition to the Brotherhood of the Oppressed.

Mohammed Rehib was the leader, and to give his life for his country was a small price to pay to injure America with the warheads. The fourth wave of Strings saw the ship and fired.

Terran's men aboard the ship began firing back with the fifty-caliber mounts on the top deck. Two Strings went down; the other seven recircled and began firing. They crippled the medium-sized ship. The Brothers of the Oppressed, seeing help had arrived, simultaneously began firing at the fourth wave of Strings who quickly pulled up. The first three waves circled and hit again. The bullets were like a lead rainfall on the brothers, yet they weathered the storm. After each String made two assaults, they headed to Hayward Airport, which was closed for military use. There they refueled and reloaded arms. The general in charge pulled the remaining waves back to reevaluate logistics. The decision was to send a wave of nine Strings every five hours to pinpoint targets.

Hours later, as the firing stopped and no visible aircraft was visible, the crew from the Middle East was able to get out thirty huge rafts and bring more supplies to the oppressed. They were in desperate need of food, ammunition, and more men. Specks, a narrow black-skinned individual with an egg head and a scar across his left cheek, who spent twelve years behind bars for rape and murder, knew things were serious now. Over five hundred Middle Easterners with plenty of rations coming behind them from the bay meant someone was going to die. Specks, never seeing small craft like the String, was amused. "What the hell, little funny-looking ass jets, what will they think of next? Who's shooting them damn things. They are eating our ass up.

That evening, reports of the attack was on nationwide television. Through Kank's confession, it was sadly reported that Larry Williams, also known as Greydog, was one of the main instigators forming the gang considering themselves as Brotherhood of the Oppressed. The news showed clips of Larry while playing college football and a picture of him in his army uniform. The newscaster went on to say that a million-dollar reward was offered for any information leading to the location of Mr. Williams.

Three weeks passed with Operation G-force making routine flights over the area. The Brothers of the Oppressed still hadn't surrendered. Albeit patient, the government wanted control. By now, the warheads were in Los Angeles, tucked away in the semi at Recreation Park near Long Beach.

Saturday, January 16, the oppressed came out for some air. Through surveillance, the air force was contacted, and the Strings, ready to go, were taken to a high altitude and then released. Upon hearing the jets descend on them, the oppressed fired. There were eight waves, with nine Strings in each wave. The oppressed fought gallantly, but they were no match for the sharp-shooting marines. You could hear the screams as the bullets riddled flesh, the all-too-familiar sickening sounds of war. Thousands of dead bodies now lay on the streets of Alameda. The oppressed were hurting, yet they still refused to give up. Specks, still alive, couldn't help but fear for his life now. He sobbed to Wobbly one morning as they dragged the dead bodies to the beach, "Why us, Wobbly, why us?" Rahib was dead; he took one in the forehead. Shortly after finding out Rahib was dead, the Middle Eastern terrorists, after consideration, all put their weapons down and walked toward the authorities near Bay Farm Island.

Specks couldn't believe it. "Those punks." With plenty of ammo and food, the Brotherhood of the Oppressed wasn't going to quit. Knowing that Kank spilled the beans, they began to weaken. Only twenty thousand members were capable of fighting now, others were too maimed to make a difference. Things looked bleak for the oppressed.

The airmen and marines were ecstatic, only twelve Strings were lost. The dead servicemen would be greatly missed, yet victory was sweet to the survivors.

As the Middle Eastern warriors were rounded up, an interpreter had to be called in to understand what the men were saying. Raheed Telihiv was a tough, hard-nosed, but small Iranian who'd been promised money and no more jail time to help with the war on America. The interpreter, a black ex-Muslim, now a Central Intelligence agent who spoke almost a half a dozen languages, was tough on Raheed.

Johnny, Thomas, Alhad Taheesh, his Muslim name, was sickened by the terrorists' feeble attempt to destroy America. He was a large man with bulging eyes and a large nose that reminded one of the pure African blood racing through those veins. His acne-scarred face was the only thing about him that gave away his heritage of being a Negroid. In the Arabic tongue, Johnny beat Raheed again, asking him, "Who sent you!" There was silence. Again, Raheed was beaten. After ten minutes of this, Raheed was barely conscious. He finally raised his hand in surrender. Johnny stopped the beating. As the agents stood over Raheed, they listened in shock as Raheed, after spitting out teeth, informed the agents that nuclear bombs were going to cripple America. Raheed went on to say that he didn't know where the bombs were located. He then laughed a sharp haunting laugh. Agent Thomas, out of anger, slit Raheed's throat in front of five other prisoners waiting to be questioned. The other five hundred men were held at the old army base that the Brotherhood of the Oppressed had used. Then Murhan Surdah spoke up, "I know where the bombs are, but they have a timer that will detonate automatically." Surdah, a petty criminal who had dreams of going back to his family after the war, never dreamed America would be this tough. He was told back home that Americans were soft. Before the agent could strike Surdah, the governor stepped in. "Enough, Agent." He then ordered the terrorists to be locked up in separate cells until further investigation. Right now, the governor was going to inform Washington.

With the gang being cut down to half strength, Specks and Wobbly were the only leaders left. Jackal, Senile, Skeeter, and Mookie were down, slain by those monstrous little blue jets that rained from the sky.

Sunday, January 31, the year 2006 started as shaky as any New Year ever on American soil. News of the attempted takeover was reported all over the world. The accounts of the bomb had not been reported yet; no need to upset an already-shaken public.

The president, being informed by Governor Bryant, knew that the bombs were in the Los Angeles area. The president had no other recourse but to inform the special nuclear team called NEST, Nuclear Emergency Support Team. This volunteer army of people with special skills knew they had their work cut out for them, searching Los Angeles. The group called six hundred members for deployment. The crew was ready.

They sent out twelve teams of helicopters, complete with high-tech sniffing devices to scan the Los Angeles area. These instruments in the helicopters were valuable tools to NEST. They picked up radiation on the ground. Searching wouldn't be easy with radiation coming from several sources, including hospitals that are stacked with radioactive materials for cancer treatment and medical test. Other radiation-emitting objects were granite and other stones. NEST scientists did have a powerful tool on their side. Using detectors linked to huge mainframe computer databases, they would scan spectrographs readouts of the energy of radioactive waves to determine the unique fingerprints of the radiation sources. They still had to have a little luck on their side. They scanned the Los Angeles area for three days. They found the Cal's Produce trailer unhitched to a tractor. Careful not to open the trailer door, a hole was cut in the roof of the trailer. The nuclear devices had been discovered. Though the bombs were of the old variety, they still would have packed a devastating blow. Possibly three quarters of America would have been affected. The bombs were deactivated, and the air force thanked their lucky stars.

February 4, Thursday, the Brothers of the Oppressed slowly began to trickle down the road to surrender. The G-Strings traveling in waves of four received some resistance, yet the fight was knocked out of the oppressed. With only one thousand Brothers of the Oppressed left, the government decided they would make G-String sweeps every hour until total submission.

Specks was now one of two leaders left in charge of the withered gang. Specks vowed to die for the cause of oppression, yet his followers had other plans. That evening, when no Strings were flying overhead, the oppressed ran for the authorities. Wobbly, now with only fifty men, had one last round in his blowpipe shoulder assault weapon. With the gang saying there was no one left to fight, the air force was notified. The president, not to be fooled, ordered the Strings to keep making waves. The six thousand Strings were a tad much, but officials couldn't be too sure with all the chaos going on in the world. On the last wave, February 11, Friday, the Strings fired indiscriminately into the homes where the gang was thought to be occupying. The marines, smelling blood now, wanted to end the monthlong battle. Wobbly was nicked in the leg. Crippled now, he crawled outside of the battle-torn home he was shelled up in; and with blowpipe in hand, he found a target and fired, and it connected. He hit craft X714. "X741 down, X741 down, will head to San Francisco Bay, abandon craft there, over and out." Another wave spotted the shooter. Wobbly was hit with dozens of rounds; he left this life in pieces. When the bullets stopped, the remaining ten members of the Brothers of the Oppressed, including Specks, ran toward the authorities to give up. X741 had been nicked in the rear by Wobbly's missile. The four men, the air force lieutenant, and three marine lance corporals were pulled safely out of the water by the Coast Guard. The miniature inflatable life jackets came in handy. One thousand of the Strings had been in actual combat. Some were in bad need of repair, yet the air force was so satisfied with Cade's idea that they planned the use of the craft in the next skirmish.

The United States Army had been called in to make a sweep of the area the gang had taken over to wage war in. The soldiers, in full combat gear, found no gang members hiding during the two-day search. Over twenty thousand army infantry men had been called in. The infiltration had been squashed. Now the burdensome task to remove some twenty-five thousand corpses was at hand. The stench could be smelled throughout Alameda, yet victory smelled sweeter to the American public.

The military realized that twenty G-Strings were destroyed and—including airmen, marines, national guardsmen, and law officers—some five hundred armed men of justice went down. The nation mourned the loss of its heroes.

By Tuesday, February 15, John was relaxing in the specially equipped patio of his new home in Northside, Chicago. The patio was all glass, and it allowed John to warmly view the chilly outdoors of a wintry Chicago. John wanted to relax for a spell; he had grown tired of all the phone calls. "John, come over here,"

Carolyn said as she stepped out on to the patio observing her honey. "Hey, Carolyn, been thinking about you. What's up?"

"You know what's up, hold out your finger," Carolyn teased. "I have something for you." John, as he stood up, walked over to Carolyn and watched her hold out a ring, a large diamond-studded platinum affair. "Something for America's hero." Before she could slip the ring on, there was a phone call, and it was the Atlanta Falcons. Carolyn, still in her uniform, wiggled over to the phone. John, still observing Carolyn's backside, couldn't help but to appreciate those hips in the crisp-cut uniform. He silently sang, "Air force blue."

www.ingramcontent.com/pod-product-compliance
Lightning Source LLC
LaVergne TN
LVHW061548070526
838199LV00077B/6951